"Just one more night—back then I wanted you so much I could taste it," Renny said.

"A farewell performance?" Jacqueline asked lightly.

Was she laughing at him? He had no way of knowing, and it made him crazy. "That's a terrible thing to call it, but since you did, and I never got it, how about a welcome home?"

He dragged her tightly against him, bent and took her lips with a kind of desperate tenderness, a growl of frustration rumbling in his throat when she resisted him. When he grew more insistent, she tossed her head to escape his kiss.

Moving was her biggest mistake. She knew it at once, but the sensation of his mouth stroking over her face was too sweet to resist. She continued moving out of his range, but more and more slowly, more sensuously. They both knew she no more wanted out of that embrace than he did. His lips touched her everywhere—her temple, her cheeks, her chin. His fingers tangled in her hair as his lips nibbled her neck in a slow dance that set her blood aflame . . .

WHAT ARE *LOVESWEPT* ROMANCES?

They are stories of true romance and touching emotion. We believe those two very important ingredients are constants in our highly sensual and very believable stories in the *LOVESWEPT* line. Our goal is to give you, the reader, stories of consistently high quality that may sometimes make you laugh, sometimes make you cry, but are always fresh and creative and contain many delightful surprises within their pages.

Most romance fans read an enormous number of books. Those they truly love, they keep. Others may be traded with friends and soon forgotten. We hope that each *LOVESWEPT* romance will be a treasure—a "keeper." We will always try to publish

LOVE STORIES YOU'LL NEVER FORGET
BY AUTHORS YOU'LL ALWAYS REMEMBER

The Editors

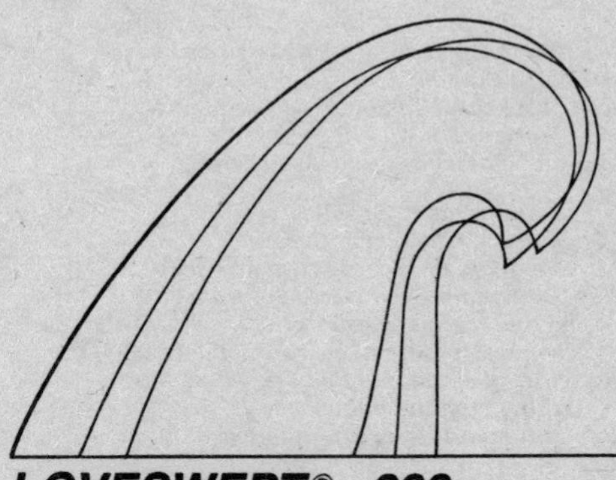

LOVESWEPT® • 282

Judy Gill

Renegade

BANTAM BOOKS
TORONTO • NEW YORK • LONDON • SYDNEY • AUCKLAND

RENEGADE

A Bantam Book / October 1988

If you would be interested in receiving protective vinyl covers for your Loveswept books, please write to this address for information:

Loveswept
Bantam Books
P. O. Box 985
Hicksville, NY 11802

ISBN 0-553-21936-7

Published simultaneously in the United States and Canada

Bantam Books are published by Bantam Books, a division of Bantam Doubleday Dell Publishing Group, Inc. Its trademark, consisting of the words "Bantam Books" and the portrayal of a rooster, is Registered in U.S. Patent and Trademark Office and in other countries. Marca Registrada. Bantam Books, 666 Fifth Avenue, New York, New York 10103.

PRINTED IN THE UNITED STATES OF AMERICA

O 0 9 8 7 6 5 4 3 2 1

For Meghan Desirée—
welcome to the world, baby.
April 9, 1988

One

Now that daylight had arrived Renny Knight could see the area that he'd been driving through for the past hour. The Selkirk Mountains loomed all around, in the west lit gold and pink, in the east still, black shapes with a fiery, cloud-dotted sky behind them. Deep in the valleys long, fjordlike lakes gleamed dully, as cascading streams, ice-flanked and frothing, tumbled into them and then snaked out into fir-shaded forests.

As he swung the truck in a wide curve around a granite-lined cliff, Ren slowed and came to a stop, his eyes widening in appreciation of what lay before him. It was a triangular valley, the twin mountains at either end of the base appearing to have been swept aside by the hands of nature to provide a better view of the massif at the triangle's apex. That sweeping motion had created a valley with sloping sides that rose in uneven terraces north and south and, at the western end, where the valley narrowed, stood what he guessed must be his destination—Roseate Mountain. It lived up to its name, he decided.

Impatient to end his journey Ren drove on toward the buildings he could see, their windows winking brightly against the snow-covered land. It was going to be good to have snow under his feet again and mountains in his view. *If he stayed.* The thought came to mind suddenly, and he brushed it aside. He meant to stay only long enough to find the answers to a couple of questions, one being why he had felt such a burning need to make the trip in the first place. Then, as always, he'd be on the road again—a new road, a new destination, a new adventure. If he wanted mountains and snow, he could find them, bigger and better, in a lot more exciting places than this.

He parked at the end of a row of cars and stepped out into the crisp air, seeing the moving chairs of a ski lift swing up and out of their shed to sail aloft empty. Tracks on the snow, however, suggested that someone was up on the slope, and he scanned the mountain, searching. A flash of brilliant color caught his attention and blinked out of sight before he could focus on it. It came into view again, much lower down, and he distinguished a skier dressed in a scarlet suit, flying over the snow, eating up distance, expertly maneuvering with a grace and skill that was pure joy to witness.

Joy, too, was in the verve with which the skier moved, the energy, the exuberance as she took to the air again and again, flying from hillock to hillock, skis touching down in perfect alignment each time, speed growing with each passing moment as she headed toward the lip of a sharp-sided bowl which, if filled with liquid, would be spilling directly onto Ren. It could, he saw, be entered by only two routes. The easiest of those was a gentle, shallow trough on the left. The other was a treacherous run that would force the skier to slalom among the pylons of the chairlift towers and many clumps of trees. He laughed softly, his breath leaving puffs of white vapor in the air. He knew exactly which route his scarlet skier would pick, just as he knew exactly who was wearing that suit.

Jacqueline! An unexpected surge jolted through him. His brows lifted in surprise as she bypassed the top of the challenging run and angled her way across the slope, letting her momentum carry her far around the top edge of the bowl, where she was momentarily swallowed up by a fold of land. She reappeared almost at once, her speed having doubled as she crouched low over her skis, heading straight toward the cliff at the top of the bowl, as if she were a scarlet bullet which, once fired, was powerless to change its own trajectory.

At the very brink, she arose from her tuck and stretched herself out over her skis, soaring up and up, claiming the air as her element. Out, out, out she flew, steady and lovely in a flight that seemed to take endless moments. She was a poem, a song, as she hovered there and was captured for all time in Ren's memory as a still photograph.

When her skis kissed the snow again, her landing looked as gentle and as easy as a sea gull alighting on a wave, and she was in perfect control as she rushed toward him across the pristine whiteness of the snow.

Renny! Jacqueline saw him as soon as she landed. Her reaction to his appearance surprised her. Her heart suddenly stopped, then started up again slowly, painfully. Inside her heavy leather gloves, her palms grew moist. A bead of sweat rolled between her breasts. He was as tall as she remembered. His shoulders, within the confines of his sheepskin jacket, were as broad. Her memory hadn't exaggerated one little bit, as she had so often told herself it had. His hair, as dark as her own, curled carelessly across his forehead over thick brows. His hands were stuffed into his pockets, and his big feet were planted apart as he stood watching her approach. She bit her lip and steadied herself—inside and out—and when she came to a neat halt close to him, she was under firm control.

Pushing her goggles up to the front of her red hat, she tilted her head back and smiled at him. "Good morning, Ren," she said, as if it hadn't been more than two years since she had seen him. "What a surprise."

He lifted one dark brow as he smiled at her. "Is

it? Funny. You don't look surprised. Though I thought, for once, maybe you would."

Her smile turned to a grin. "Sorry to disappoint you." If only he knew! She hadn't had the slightest clue that he was back.

His white teeth glittered in the early morning light. "Oh, but you haven't. I'd be disappointed if you did what was expected of you. You always managed to keep life interesting."

"What a relief! I'd hate to think I might have bored you, Renny," she said dryly. "I've never cared to be just one of the crowd." Her smile faded as she heard the slightly antagonistic note in her voice. With a grimace of annoyance, she planted her poles into the snow and pushed off, ski-skating hard and fast away from him, knowing without looking back that he was following her at a seemingly leisurely pace but nevertheless was covering a lot of territory in a big hurry.

She had her skis clipped together and leaning in a rack when he reached her side. She pulled off her goggles and knit hat and shoved a hand through her short, curly hair.

Her hair had been long and straight last time he'd seen it, a dusky curtain that could cover her dark pink nipples, and had, Ren recalled. The memory of how he had parted that curtain with his hands flooded unexpectedly over him, and when she spoke, it jarred him back to the present with an unpleasant thud.

With a cool smile, she said, "Did you have a

nice trip, Ren? Plenty of new places, new faces? Lots of adventure?"

He nodded. "It was what I wanted," he said, but knew he lied. In retrospect, he could recall plenty of times when he had known it was not what he wanted. Yet, he wasn't sure exactly what was.

"I must have missed the news of your triumphant return," she said. "If I'd known you were back, I'd have expected a phone call or a letter from your lawyer, but certainly not a personal visit from you. Still can't stand San Diego? How are your parents?"

He grinned. "Overbearing. Insufferably superior. Demanding."

She had to laugh. Those were the exact words she'd used to describe his parents after she'd supervised their fortieth wedding anniversary celebration in the San Diego hotel where she'd worked. At the time she hadn't known she was talking to their son, but he'd agreed with her wholeheartedly, and from there the beginnings of a friendship had sprung up. That their friendship had died aborning was of little concern now.

"I'm the boss now, the general manager of this resort. So I no longer permit myself even to think such things about my guests, let alone say them. I'm sure your parents have many redeeming features."

"I haven't been able to find them. So, characteristically, I split after a month of trying. And here I am."

"So I see," she said blandly. "What do you want here, Ren?"

He looked at her. What, exactly, did he want here? Her face was lovely in the winter sunlight, her skin almost transparent. Her dispassionate tone was belied by the watchful, almost wary look in her eyes.

He could be just as cool. "For starters, how about breakfast?"

Of course, she thought. Food was one of Renny Knight's greatest pleasures, and he had never been a man to deny himself anything. As she'd made her way down on the last of her three morning runs, she'd been thinking of food herself. Now, though, her appetite seemed to have disappeared. She felt slightly sick, she had to admit. His sudden appearance had unnerved her badly. She had never expected to see him again, and now that she had, she knew she'd been right to send him away as soon as she'd freed him from his part of their bargain. She had removed him from her life before he'd had a chance to destroy it.

Unless he had merely come to ski? Though that, she decided, was pretty unlikely. After all, why would he choose a very minor ski resort that was well off the beaten track, tucked away in a secluded valley in British Columbia? It was not Renny Knight's style. This place would never hold him, she realized, nothing would.

Which was why she had chosen him, she reminded herself. He was a wanderer. It wasn't his fault that she'd done the unthinkable and fallen in love with him.

"This way," she said, and swung away from him.

He caught her arm. "Jac?" He turned her to face him. He watched her expression, searching for emotion, should there be any, but of course there wasn't. Jacqueline's aqua eyes were clear and serene, betraying nothing of what she might be feeling, assuming she felt anything at all toward him—and that she might was a pretty farfetched assumption, he told himself. Jacqueline Train showed none of her feelings. Jacqueline Train did not acknowledge emotions as part of her makeup. Jacqueline Train was so totally self-sufficient that she never needed anyone—yet once she had needed him.

Him? No. Almost any man could have given her what she wanted—had thought she'd wanted. It was just the luck of the draw that he had been in the right place at the right time and had needed something she could provide in return. There had been nothing personal in it, on his part or on hers. Yet he had made her eyes glaze with pleasure. He had made her feel passion. She had been unable to hide her reactions to his touch. In fairness, he had to admit she hadn't tried to hide those reactions any more than he had.

He swallowed hard to rid himself of the thickness in his throat. So why had there been a hint of bitterness in the words she had spoken? Had she felt something, even pique, when he'd left so willingly—at her suggestion, he reminded himself. *I'd hate to think I might have bored you. . . .* Was that what she thought she'd done? He frowned, and lifted a hand to flick away a melted snowflake that lay on her soft cheek like a crystal teardrop. Tears. Had Jacqueline shed any tears for him?

"Jac?"

She looked at him. His eyes were the same intense blue she had never tried to forget. Why try to forget? There were some memories, experience had taught her, that refused to be eradicated, and Renny Knight played a major part in them. She hadn't expected to see him again, so what harm could there be in remembering? Only now he was here, and it was hard to maintain a façade of indifference.

His lips were firm and a shade paler than the dark tan of his face. His cheeks were hollow, and his jaw had the same stubborn thrust she had admired the moment she'd met him. Their first few conversations had shown him to be a man of convictions, a man of character with obvious strengths, both inner and outer. Like her, he had known what he wanted and was determined to get it—any way he could.

She managed not to flinch when he touched her cheek. She made stepping back from him seem casual and natural, but his touch on her face, as brief and as soft as it had been, stirred her deeply, softening her insides as no other man had ever been able to do. One touch! Oh, heaven help her, she realized. One little touch!

"Jac, *you* never bored me," he said softly, his breath puffing out white and vaporous.

She wished she could think of something snappy to say, something quick and cute and smart to make him smile, to wipe those words from his mind. She must have been out of hers, letting him see that moment of vulnerability. But she had no riposte, and she still felt oddly vulnerable.

"Did I bore you?" he asked.

Slowly, she shook her head, and managed to smile again. "What? In six weeks? It was hardly time to get to know you, let alone become bored with you."

"I remember," he said, his voice a low rumble. "There are lots of things about those six weeks that I never forgot. I used to think about that time we spent together, Jac, out there on the ocean. I wondered about you and—and what was happening in your life."

"We had—have—an agreement, Ren," she said sharply. "I stuck to my half of the bargain, and I released you from yours."

She faced him, challenge in her expression, in her stance. He met her gaze. She was right. He had agreed not to interfere in her life, but then, he hadn't even considered that he might like to know how things had worked out for her, hadn't considered that he'd never be able to get her out of his mind.

He had time. His long days at sea had taught him patience. He'd simply stay and explore his feelings for her—or exorcise them once and for all.

He'd reflected that if he'd had patience before, in their earlier relationship, he might have left knowing more about Jacqueline Train than the skeletal information she had provided: Parents—dead. Brothers and sisters—none. Aunts, uncles, grandparents—the same.

Then, he had envied her.

Except once in a while when he sensed a terrible, yearning loneliness in her, one that she tried to hide by pretending to need no one. Well, not quite no one. He had tried to get her to talk, but she'd managed to change the subject each time, or to evade his questions in some other way, or simply to silence them with a cold, unforgiving glare that made him feel like a snoop, an intruder, a worm of the lowest order. Instead of continuing to probe, he'd told himself he didn't give a damn about what made her tick—only he had.

Again, it had taken until he was isolated with his own thoughts far from shore, with no human contact, for him to begin to sort through feelings and memories. Always, it was the memories of Jacqueline Train that had come the strongest, the most often.

"If you came hoping to ski, Ren, I'm sorry to tell you that we aren't open yet," she said, breaking in on his ruminations.

"I came for more than skiing," he admitted

slowly. "I came to see you. I think we have unfinished business, Jacqueline."

"Sorry, you're wrong."

He withdrew a newspaper clipping from his pocket, unfolded it, and held it out to her. Until this moment he hadn't been sure why he'd brought it with him, but now it was about to come in handy, he decided.

She gazed at it, at the picture of herself, the words underneath. "Where did you get this? It was published over a year ago."

"And reprinted two months back in a series on women in business."

"So I see. What's your point?"

"The name, Jacqueline. The name."

She lifted her brows. "I don't recall any rules regarding names."

"Jacquie, sorry to interrupt," her maintenance chief said, "but the government guy's coming this morning at ten to inspect the lifts. Will you want to see him?" She turned and gave him a quick smile.

"Hi, Bill. No, that's okay. You can handle it. Of course, if he wants to see me, I'll be in my office. Just give me a call."

"Yes, ma'am." Bill stamped his booted feet in the cold, cupped his ungloved hands and blew into them. He looked curiously from Jacquie to Renny.

She sighed. She didn't have much choice, did she?

"Bill, this is Renny Knight. Ren, Bill Howe."

The two men shook hands. "Knight? Any relation?"

"No," said Jacqueline.

"Husband," said Ren.

"I—uh—yeah. Nice meeting you, Mr. Knight."

"Sure, Bill. Call me Ren."

"Ren." With a last, confused look from Jacquie to Ren, Bill Howe stomped away toward the lift.

"What did you do that for?"

"What?" Ren fell into step beside her, shortening his paces to match hers as she clunked down the steps toward the basement of the day lodge and the cafeteria.

"Oh, don't give me the innocent act. Why did you introduce yourself as my husband?"

"Because that's what I am." He opened the door, holding it while she walked inside, and then slid onto a bench beside her as she sat down. He patted the pocket where he had replaced the clipping. "Seems you've been using my name, making it public that you're my wife. Why shouldn't I introduce myself as your husband?"

"Because you're not," she said, bending down to unsnap the buckle at the back of one of her ski boots. He lifted her other boot onto his thigh and undid it, pulling it off and setting it beside its mate.

"These yours?" he asked, reaching for a pair of shaggy mukluks. Without waiting for an answer, he slipped one of the soft-soled boots onto her foot.

Gritting her teeth, Jacquie swung half-around

and stuffed her other foot into the soft warmth of the other fur-lined boot. She was letting him get to her, and she simply had to stop it. Standing, she unzipped her one-piece ski suit to the waist, pulled her arms free, and left the top hanging down her back. She was intensely aware of his gaze on her high, full breasts, which were clearly outlined by the fabric of her black turtleneck sweater.

She cleared her throat. He lifted his gaze to hers, smiling in appreciation, then let it wander again to where her zipper tab hung, six inches from the end of its track. His fingers twitched.

"Don't even think about it," she said.

He laughed softly. "Why not? You can't hang a guy for his thoughts. Anyway, how did you know I was wondering what would happen if I pulled that zipper to its lowest limit? Am I so transparent?"

"Sometimes," she said. "And if you tried it, you'd find out what a fast and effective knee reflex I have."

He grinned. "What did you mean, I'm not your husband?" he asked, following her as she marched to the counter where breakfast was laid out.

"Renny. Not here," she said in a fierce whisper, grabbing a plate and ladling scrambled eggs onto it. She added a couple of slices of bacon, then some toast, and poured herself a cup of coffee. Ren reached over her shoulder and added a glass of frothy orange juice.

"Vitamins," he said. Jacquie only took her tray and sailed back to the table, her head held high.

Behind her, she heard Elsie, the cashier, say to Ren, "Two fifty-five, please."

"Is that for me and my wife?" he asked.

Jacquie slammed her tray onto the table, slopping coffee and orange juice into her plate. She didn't have to turn around to know that Elsie was staring at Ren.

"Wife?" Elsie's voice rose to a squeak. "You're Jacquie's husband? Well! So you're real. A lot of us have been wondering about you, even though her secretary's been drooling over your photograph on Jacquie's desk. Welcome to Roseate Mountain, and of course you don't have to pay for your breakfast—or any other meal in this cafeteria. I'm Elsie, and whenever you want something to eat, you just come and ask for me, Mr. Knight."

"Call me Ren." Jacquie guessed he was treating Elsie to one of his rogue smiles, the kind of smile that could melt the socks off any woman—socks and whatever else he might want off her.

"Elsie," she said sternly, swiveling around in her chair. "He eats, he pays. And don't you go tempting him to stick around. He won't be staying long."

"Oh, Jacquie!" Elsie said, her round eyes nearly closing in creases of fat as she laughed. "He's your own husband, and you're pretending to rush him off. What a kidder you are!"

"Isn't she?" said Ren with a chuckle. "Always was. That was the very thing I missed most while I was at sea, Jacquie's kidding."

It was Elsie's turn to chuckle again. "Oh, sure. I'll bet it was."

She and Ren shared a grin that would have made Jacquie blush had she been the blushing kind. Instead, she compressed her lips into a severe frown.

Turning back in her chair, Jacquie stared in distaste at the mingling brown and orange liquid additions to her eggs and shoved the tray away in disgust. She took her coffee cup from it and sipped, nearly choking when she heard Ren add, "But now that I'm home, I plan to stay, Elsie, and if the rest of your meals look as appetizing as this, you won't be able to keep me out of your cafeteria."

Plan to stay? The words echoed in Ren's mind as he walked to the table where Jacquie sat. Did he? He looked at her. Without his knowing it, his mind had been made up. Yes. He planned to stay. For a while.

One slice of her toast was edible, and Jacquie nibbled at that between sips of coffee, pointedly ignoring the orange juice, just as pointedly as she ignored the man who sat across from her cheerfully consuming great gobs of scrambled eggs. How did he do it? He ate like a logger and had the lean, powerful physique of a male figure skater. She knew how he did it. He burned it all off during sex!

When he was finished, he wiped his mouth on a napkin, leaned back, and looked at Jacquie. His lips curved into a smile. His eyes held a glint of laughter. "Now," he said, "what did you mean? Am I, or am I not your husband?"

"Not," she said succinctly, setting her cup back onto the tray with a decisive click. Shoving her arms back into the top half of her ski suit, she shrugged it over her shoulders and stood, then gathered up her ski boots.

"If you'll excuse me now, I have to get to work. Nice seeing you again, Renny. Good of you to drop by. Why don't you do it again in another couple of years? But make reservations first, okay? The lodge isn't due to open for another three days, and when it does, we're booked solid."

"Jacqueline, we have things to discuss."

"I'll sign any papers your lawyer sends me. There's no need for you to bring them. We have nothing to discuss," she reiterated firmly and walked away—quickly, before she disgraced herself.

Two

"Dammit, nobody walks away from Renny Knight," he muttered, and took three large steps, following her. The swinging door nearly caught him in the face. This time, his mutter was louder and considerably more profane, but he shoved the door the other way and caught up with her in the basement foyer, grabbing her by one shoulder and spinning her around before she could mount the stairs.

His eyes weren't full of laughter now. He wasn't smiling.

Neither was she. "What do you want?"

"To talk to you."

"All right then, talk. But if you want to talk about what I think you want to talk about, then don't expect any response. I'll listen." She popped her wrist free of her cuff and glanced at her watch.

"For two minutes. But my life is mine, Renny Knight, and you have no right to question me about it."

"Why?" His hand touched her cheek, slid to her chin. She continued to look at him, her expression cool and quiet. She would not show him that his touch was converting her insides to mush.

As she remained still, refusing to give him the satisfaction of seeing her flinch, his hand trailed down her throat, the backs of his fingers caressing her. One thumbnail scraped on her zipper, following its path down as his fingers brushed over the rise of her breasts, followed the contours of her shape to the narrowness of her waist and the tab of the zipper. He clasped the tab, his gaze on hers. Inside her, something began to throb, to grow, to burn, and she clamped her teeth together, hard. For just a moment, his hand slipped inside her ski suit, his palm hot and hard through the fabric of her sweater. He tucked the material out of the way and then withdrew his hand to pull her zipper up and over her breasts.

"You forgot to do up your suit. It's cold outside."

She tilted her head to one side and smiled. "Is that what you wanted to talk about? Thank you," she said with mock solemnity. "I hadn't noticed. And now, since that seems to be all you have to say, and since your time is up, I'm leaving. Goodbye, Ren."

Jacquie's secretary, Mai, stamped snow off her boots as she came down the stairs. "Hi, Jac. Have I got time to grab something to eat before I come up to the office? The kids were slow this morning." Her gaze wasn't on Jacquie; it was on the tall man who stood closer to her boss than any man had ever dared to do in Mai's experience. What had happened to the invisible circle Jacquie always drew around her? This man either couldn't see it or was ignoring it.

Suddenly, she recognized the sheepskin-coated guy as the smiling, centerfold-handsome man on the deck of a sailboat in the picture Jacquie kept on her desk.

"Oh!" she said. "Oh, he's come back! Jacquie, how wonderful for you!" Impulsively she hugged her boss. "I'll bring you coffee, okay? Both of you? Oh, if only it could be champagne!"

"Coffee," said Jacqueline firmly, disentangling herself from her secretary's embrace. "Just coffee, Mai. For me." With a final, cool glance at Ren, she mounted the stairs and walked away, swinging her boots from her left hand as if she weren't in danger of falling apart. He must never know. Never. She was still in love with him. It hadn't died a natural death, the love that should never have been born in the first place. It had lain dormant, until he came back and brought it to life with a smile, a touch, the sound of his voice. And it hurt!

At the top of the stairs, she turned and looked down. He was watching her as she knew he would be.

"Good-bye," she said clearly, once more, as she had that day two years before from the deck of his friend's power cruiser. With the rumble of the heavy diesels and the whistle of the wind in his ears, he hadn't heard her, but he had seen the shape of the word on her lips, he remembered.

Now, as he had that day, he responded automatically. "See you," he said.

This time, he meant it.

He had to find out what was going on. Why she was so antagonistic.

"Jacquie? Jacqueline? Are you okay?"

She took her hands away from her face and smiled at Mai.

"Sure. I'm fine. You brought my coffee," she added gratefully. "Thanks, Mai. But I could have waited for our own pot to brew."

"I also brought your juice. Ren said you should drink it. He thinks you look pale."

Jacquie laughed. "Would you bring me the file on our high school ski clubs? I have an idea I want to explore, and I need to see what some of the costs were for the groups in past years. Maybe we can save them some money."

With a questioning look, Mai complied, and Jacquie spent the rest of the day immersed in work. She ate lunch at her desk, passed up her usual afternoon runs, and continued until long after Mai had gone home. It was nearly seven when she rose from her desk, stretched, and grabbed her jacket. Kicking off her shoes, she put on her mukluks and went still at the memory of

Ren's hand around her foot when he put her boot on for her earlier. Then she was reminded of his touch on her cheek and her reaction to it, and the way he had let his hand trail down her zipper and had slipped his palm inside her ski suit. She swallowed.

Dammit, she had to stop this! She was not going to give in to the memories that had plagued her during the first few days after Renny Knight had sailed happily out of her life. So he had touched something in her that had never been touched before, elicited responses from her that she hadn't believed herself capable of giving, found a soft core of womanliness underneath her strong exterior that she had never wanted exposed. That didn't mean she had to succumb to thoughts of him just because he had popped his head back into her life for half an hour this morning. She had told him to get lost, and since the day had gone by with no more sign of him, presumably he had. Which was good, she realized. There was no more room for him in her life now than there had been two years ago. She couldn't understand why he had come back to see her. He had no room in his life for her either.

She locked up her office and made her way down the back stairs of the administration building, glancing around automatically to be sure everything was as it should be. Here and there, people moved from building to building; workers heading toward dinner in the cafeteria, to the staff quarters in the building she had just left, or to their cars in the parking lot and the drive down the mountain to Marsden, the nearest town.

On her left, the lodge was quiet, the windows dark. In three days, in time for Thanksgiving—American Thanksgiving, the Canadian holiday of the same name having been in October—it would be filled, the windows sending glowing light across the snow. Since the lodge was so close to the border and Idaho, most of their guests would be Americans who were happy to bring their stronger dollar here, which was the reason Captain Harbison, her boss, had bought the place.

The windows of the lodge were beginning to catch glimmers of the moon as it rose over the mountain range. The twenty-one chalets, invisible now without lights or occupants, were nestled in the trees at the edge of the forest a quarter mile away. She headed toward them, her feet crunching in the crispness of snow.

After a near collision with a couple of very young dining room trainees, Jacquie discovered they were using serving trays as sleds.

"Gentlemen," she said sternly, "I suggest you get these trays back into the dining room without François seeing them. Believe me, if push comes to shove, I'd find it a whole lot easier to replace two busboys than I would one French chef. Got it?"

"Yes, ma'am," one boy said.

"Sure, Mrs. Knight. Sorry," said the other.

"Okay. Now get out of here before I get phone calls from your moms about sending you driving down the mountain so late. But first, how did your training session go?"

"Okay." Robby answered for both. "I guess it'll be a lot different when there are real customers in the dining room, though."

"Count on it," said Jacquie, a note of warning in her voice. "Night, boys. Here's a word of advice from an old-time resort rat—inner tubes make much better sleds than trays do."

They're so young, she thought. But at least the two of them still lived at home and went to school. Many of the others didn't and didn't look or act old enough to be away from home. Then, who was she to talk?

Since the age of sixteen, she had been on her own, with the exception of the six weeks she had lived with Ren. She mentally shook off what threatened to be another rush of debilitating memories and quickened her pace.

Her chalet, set apart from the others in its own little grove of trees, was beckoning her, the light she had left on that morning gleaming faintly to welcome her home.

It was cold inside, and she quickly turned up the thermostat on the wall and lit the fire in the stove. Then, having put on a pot of stew for her dinner, she went into the small bathroom to run a bath—her most beloved ritual.

When the tub was filled, with a groan of pleasure, she eased her tired body into the deep, hot water and lay back. Fragrant bubbles rose up under her chin, popping, tingling, and she closed her eyes, trying to relax, breathing deeply and quietly, the morning's events replaying in her mind, unable now, or maybe just unwilling, to try to block them.

Why had he come? The question was foremost in her mind. His having the newspaper clipping didn't tell her a lot. So she had claimed him as her husband, in effect hidden behind him, used his name. By law she was entitled to use it. What difference could that make to his life? None that she could see.

Lifting her soapy sponge, she washed herself and then lay back again until the water began to cool. Reluctant to get out, she added more hot water. She should have gone to the pool. Tonight of all nights she would have benefited from its seclusion and its serenity, the relaxing properties of its minerals.

Renny . . . Wishing she could forget those blue eyes that had gazed so warmly into hers was useless, so Jacquie succumbed, thinking about Renny until she was startled into alertness by his voice calling her name.

"Jacquie? Jacqueline! Where are you?"

Why was he here? He had no right to walk into her house! Nor, she thought a second later, did he have the right to walk into her bathroom!

"Good evening," she said quietly, determined not to let him get her goat, not to let him know what his presence did to her body. "What do you want?"

She was glad that her bubbles had not completely dissipated, but they were quietly bursting away, leaving her pink-tipped breasts half-exposed and visible through the water. "I thought we'd agreed there was nothing to discuss, no reason for you to stay."

"I don't remember agreeing to any such thing. You told me there was nothing to discuss. That doesn't mean I feel the same."

He sat down and stretched his long legs out in front of him, crossing them at the ankles. He swept a glance over her. "You're just as good to look at now as you were two years ago." He seemed to be addressing not her, but her breasts.

Jacquie restrained her impulse to cover them with her hands. *Damned if I'll act like some kind of Victorian maiden!* she told herself, dismayed at how much his gaze was affecting her pulse and respiration, to say nothing of her blood pressure.

"Your dinner's ready," he said, sliding his gaze back to her face with obvious reluctance.

"Thank you," she said. "How kind of you to let me know." She had forgotten she'd put the stew on. Suddenly, she'd had enough—more than enough. "Now get out of here so I can get ready for my dinner."

"Not until we've had a chance to talk," he said, grinning down at her, clearly enjoying her discomfort. "I respected your working hours, didn't bother you all day." He frowned. "Besides, if I'd tried to see you earlier, you'd have walked away again. I don't like people to do that, Jacqueline. It irritates me. Finding you in the tub is the best luck I've had in a long while. At least I can be sure you'll stay in one place long enough for us to do a bit of talking."

He had a point there, she had to admit. While she might not want to act like a Victorian maiden, wouldn't any woman in her position draw the line at stepping naked from her tub in front of a man who, in spite of those six weeks in the past, in spite of a shared name, was still a stranger?

"Really?" She lifted her finely arched brows, drew in a deep breath, and stood, water streaming from her naked body as she stepped from the tub. Unhurriedly, she reached for a towel, wrapped it around herself, and stepped over his legs.

"Jacqueline!" His voice was hoarse as he pulled in his legs and shot to his feet, staring at her. "Damn, but you're cool!" She thought he was angry. She guessed he'd imagined that by trapping her in what to most people would have been a vulnerable position, he could get his own way.

"If you don't like it, get out of my bathroom." She laughed and began to dry herself, careful not to let the towel slip and expose any more of her body than she chose to have exposed. To do something unexpected strictly for its shock value, and to rely on that very element of shock to prevent his making a move was one thing. To leave her actions open for misinterpretation was another. She certainly did not want to give Renny Knight the wrong impression of what she might be willing to have him do.

With one more look at her, his blue eyes glittering with suppressed laughter and, she thought, a little admiration, he gave her a nod and left her alone in the bathroom. As he closed the door, the sound of his laughter floated back toward her. At least he hadn't lost his sense of humor.

When she emerged, dressed in a blue velour leisure suit, the aroma of her rich, thick stew wafted out of the kitchen. Two place settings were on the table, and Ren stood at the stove stirring the contents of the pot. He had certainly made himself at home. But then, when hadn't he? she asked herself.

With a towel over his arm, he graciously seated her at the table, heaped her plate and his, and then sat across from her. "There now," he said in a satisfied tone. "Isn't this nice? We're acting just like the real married couple you've been pretending we are."

Calmly she said, "Very nice," and proceeded to eat. She was ravenous.

Shoving her plate aside, she put her elbows on the table and looked at him, unsmiling. "All right," she said. "I guess maybe I owe you an explanation."

He lifted one brow and said, "I guess you do."

"I didn't write that article. I had no idea it would be picked up and reprinted. I thought it was going to be a local thing. I hadn't used your name until I came here. I needed it then to—to smooth my own path." She looked down, doodled with her fingernail on the tablecloth, and then glanced back up at him, contrition on her face.

He had to smile. "Hey, it's okay, really. How did

being married to me smooth your path?" he asked. "Was someone coming on to you too strong?"

She shrugged, frowned, and then nodded. "In a way, but not offensively. Just persistently. I have this old friend, Eric Sorensen. He was sort of a father figure to me for a few years when I was a child. I loved him very much, but we . . . lost touch. When I came here, to my amazement, Eric was here—is here. He's the hill manager."

"And?" Ren prompted when she fell silent, doodling on the tablecloth again. He'd met Eric today, a grizzled guy in his fifties who looked like George C. Scott.

"And he . . . well, he sort of didn't want to be a father figure to me anymore. So I brought you into the picture." She looked up, her expression earnest. "I love Eric, Ren. Please understand that. He's one of the most important people in my life, and I don't want to hurt him. But I know his feelings aren't what he likes to think they are. He's very . . . protective. He thinks that a woman needs a man to look after her. He was determined and felt the only way he could look after me properly was to marry me. I learned all this within half a day of my arrival here. I was really stuck, so I brought you into the picture and painted your position in my life as being a bit stronger than it really is. And it worked. As long as he believes I have a husband to keep me from starving if I lose my job, Eric's content to be my friend."

His next question surprised her, though it shouldn't have. She had always known that under his flippant cover of rakishness, Renny was deeply perceptive. It made him even more dangerous to her.

"And a friend is of far more value to you than a husband, isn't it?" he asked.

"Well, yes. I suppose that's true," she admitted after a moment. "But if I'd been interested in Eric that way, I'm sure I'd have accepted his proposal even though he is more than twenty years older than I am. Yet I don't want to be married. To anyone. Ever."

She seemed to be forgetting that she was speaking to her husband, Renny thought. Clearly, she didn't think of him in that role. But then, he hadn't spent a lot of time thinking of her as his wife. He had spent a lot of time thinking of her, true, but their so-called marriage hadn't figured in his thoughts. Not until he'd seen the picture of her in the newspaper article and read the name she was using—Jacqueline Knight. It had come as a bit of a shock, even made him uncomfortable, and, in spite of himself, intrigued. Not that he hadn't been wondering about her even before that; he'd spent many a night thinking he should track her down, wondering how he'd go about it. He hadn't thought she'd stay forever as assistant manager of the expensive resort where they'd met. She'd had too much on the ball.

She was one smart woman, Jacqueline Train—Knight, he reminded himself.

She smiled. "Of course, Eric's is the only offer

I've ever had, so maybe I shouldn't say so quickly that I don't want to marry."

"Not true," he said. "You had my offer. You accepted it."

"Aren't you forgetting? I was the one who did the asking."

He grinned. "I'll never forget it. I was so stunned, I refused. Then after I thought it over and decided your proposal made sense and suggested you ask me again, you were the one to refuse."

She laughed softly, a sound that sent a little curl of delight through his insides. "Whereupon you went into that ridiculous act on bended knee, hat in hand, right there in the middle of the restaurant," she remembered aloud.

He joined in her laughter, then said softly, "Ridiculous act or not, you accepted my proposal of marriage."

"That was no more a proposal of marriage than the one I had made to you," she said, getting to her feet and stacking the plates into the sink before filling their coffee cups. "What you and I had was a business arrangement for mutual benefit."

"True," he admitted, "only you changed your mind in the end." He caught her hand, pulling her close to his side. She could feel the heat of his body. "I got what I wanted out of our arrangement," he said. "I fulfilled the terms of my grandfather's will and married before my thirtieth birthday. That gave me the financing I needed to take my trip. But what about you? You didn't get the baby you wanted. You decided it wasn't the right thing to do after all. That was why you encouraged me to leave right away—because you no longer needed my . . . services."

She pulled her hand free and walked into the living area of the A-frame chalet. Standing with her palms flat on the glass at the front of the building, she stared out into the darkness. She saw his reflection behind her. His hands descended onto her shoulders. She suppressed a shudder.

"I lied to you, Ren. I was pregnant. I miscarried at four months."

Three

Renny couldn't move for a moment, shocked by her statement. Then he turned her, searching her face. As usual, it told him nothing of her feelings, but something in the way she held herself, in the rigidity of her muscles under his hands, indicated that she cared very deeply, had grieved long and bitterly—still grieved.

Gently, almost against his will, he drew her to his chest, sliding his hands down her back and then giving in to the impulse to wrap her in a tight embrace. Rocking her from side to side, he offered wordless comfort, and found himself taking comfort, too, needing it. He swallowed hard. All of a sudden, there was pain in discovering that he had created a child with Jacquie, a new life that had never really been.

She stayed rigid in his embrace for a moment

and then relaxed a bit, rubbing her cheek on his sweater. Her hair, shining and dark, gleamed in the light, and he lifted a hand, filtering the silken strands through his fingers, stroking it back from her temple, silently communicating his sympathy to her. After a long while, he said, "Something inside me sensed you hadn't given up on what you'd wanted so badly, but I also sensed you needed to get away from me. I began to believe during the last week we were together that you were very unhappy about being married to me, that you regretted being tied, if only legally, to a man you didn't love. I thought it best not to question you but to honor your request to cancel my part of the arrangement. Why didn't you tell me, Jacquie? Why didn't you want me to know you were pregnant, when that's what I'd agreed to?"

How could she tell him? How could she explain that it was because she'd fallen deeply in love with him during those few weeks that she had told him she'd changed her mind? She knew then that Renny could never follow through on his promise to let her raise the child on her own. He simply had too much love to give, and once he'd had time to think about it while alone at sea, he'd have realized the same thing and would have come back into her life—because of the child.

She'd wanted to make a clean break and had done what she'd thought was best. Ironically she'd lost the child anyway.

She gathered her courage and spoke. "I know you must think it strange that I hid the truth from you, Renny, but I was afraid you'd never be able to forget that you had a child somewhere. I know after spending time with you that you'd eventually ask to see the child, want to be a part of his or her life—and I didn't want you to be bound to us. All of us would have ended up being miserable. So I told you I'd changed my mind. A few months later I miscarried."

"What happened? Why did it happen?" he asked gently.

She drew in a deep breath and let it out, then lifted her head but didn't look at him. Tonelessly she told him, "The doctors said they didn't know. Sometimes it just happens like that."

"Were you very sick?"

"Not . . . very." Heartsick didn't count. "I was able to go back to work right away. Captain Harbison—you remember him?—promoted me to general manager and sent me here. As much as I loved the Westmount—" Her voice cracked and she swallowed hard, steadying herself. "It had been my home for six years, but I couldn't stay on there. Too many people knew. Too many people wanted me to talk about it, to cry over it, to 'let them share' what I was feeling. Lord, but I hate that phrase! I hated the pity more than I hated leaving the Westmount. No one possibly could have shared what I was feeling. No one understood."

He turned her head and looked down into her eyes. They were clear and dry. There was no sign of a tear, no sign that tears had ever filled them over the loss of her child. Yet he knew they had.

"I could have shared it," he said, surprising them both. "I would have understood." He frowned when she shook her head. "Yes. I mean it. Right now I feel something—an ache, right here." He tapped his chest. "I don't know if it's for you or me or for our child—our baby. But it's there and it hurts. Jac, I'm really, really sorry I wasn't there to share the loss with you."

Restlessly, she moved out of his embrace and walked to the couch that sat facing the fire. Curling up on one end of it, she said, "But you couldn't have shared it, Ren. It was my loss, not yours. My one chance at having someone of my very own. And you never knew about the baby, so to you, it wouldn't have been a loss."

"Why 'one' chance?" he asked. "If I had known, maybe we could have—well—tried again."

She laughed softly and shook her head. "That wasn't in the contract. You were to stay with me until I got pregnant or for one year, whichever came first. Well, I got pregnant, I just didn't tell you. It was pure good luck that it must have happened in our first week together. You'd done your bit."

For too many years he'd had to put off his dream of sailing around the world. He wondered how he would have reacted if she had told him. He'd have hated to have his trip interrupted. He'd felt so cheated when his grandfather, who had promised and promised to finance him, had kept reneging, hoping that Ren would outgrow his desire for adventure, would settle down and become the architect the old man knew he could be. But he would have been at her side in a flash, if she'd needed him—contract or no contract, he realized.

"You make it sound so cold-blooded. 'Done my bit,' " he repeated.

"Well, it was. On both our parts. It was . . . really quite horrible, don't you think? I've had time since then to become deeply ashamed of myself and of what I did. It was a lousy reason to want to bring a child into the world. *I* was lonely. *I* needed someone of my very own. *My* life was empty. Not once did I consider how a child conceived under those circumstances might feel later in life. It wasn't until after I lost the baby that I even began to think it out, to realize that maybe there was a purpose behind what had happened to me. That I was no longer pregnant because I hadn't deserved to be pregnant in the first place."

"Oh, come on!" he said in a strong voice, flopping onto the couch beside her, leaning his head back and rolling it to the side to look at her. "Do you honestly believe that? Divine retribution, or something? It's garbage, Jac! You miscarried because either your body wasn't ready to carry a child full term, or the child wasn't developing properly and Mother Nature took care of it." Desire curled in his gut as he looked at her, tightening his muscles. "I think we should try again." He lifted his head and shook it. "Was that me who said that?"

Jacquie had to laugh. "It was you. Aren't you glad I have no intention of taking you seriously?"

He cocked his head. "Haven't you?"

He experienced an odd pang of disappointment. Had he been considering, even subconsciously, trying to fulfill the rest of the terms of his grandfather's will? No. He'd never had any intention of making a claim on the balance of his inheritance. The idea had been repugnant to him then and was just as repugnant now.

"No intention at all. Didn't you hear a word I said, Ren? I conceived that child with all the wrong reasons in mind. I did it for myself, for purely selfish purposes. Not because I had something good to give to another human being, but because I wanted to feed off it, to have it love me, give me something I've always felt I was denied."

"Don't you want a child anymore?" What was he doing? he asked himself. Was he looking for an excuse to make love to her again? He swallowed hard, not taking his eyes off her, wanting her, suddenly aching from it.

She shoved her hands deep into the pockets of her velour pants and hooked her bare toes over the edge of the coffee table. Her pink polish was chipped. Oddly the slight flaw in her appearance appealed to him, made her more human. He wanted to kiss her toes—for starters. Damn! He shifted to try to loosen the pull of his pants over sensitive flesh.

She shrugged. "I don't know. But if I ever have a child, it won't be because I have a personal need to have someone of my own. I'd like to think of a child as being the result of an overwhelming love between a man and a woman. The only way they can express their love fully is to create a brand-new human being."

The thought of Jacqueline Train entertaining such a romantic notion of the way love could be was novel. It had never occurred to him that she might think along those lines. He'd assumed she was very much like he was—completely unromantic, pragmatic—and she had been. She had wanted a child but not a husband. He had wanted a marriage but not a wife. When had she changed? Did she—heaven forbid—want a husband now, to go along with her child?

Carefully he said, "So you're looking for a serious—relationship?"

"I'm not looking for a relationship. If I meet someone, great. If I don't, then I guess I've become self-sufficient enough not to need a child to make me feel complete. I know I am complete. I—I like myself a lot better than I did when we knew each other before."

When he lifted his brows questioningly, she went on, picking her words with care. "Back then I was greedy, selfish. What I wanted I wanted for myself. I would have been a bad mother. I'd probably have smothered my child. I'd have wanted to be everything to her because she was going to be everything to me."

"She? You were that positive about its sex?" Funny, when he'd thought about Jacqueline's child, he'd pictured a little boy.

"That positive. It illustrates my point. I wanted

a daughter, a little girl to become the little girl I would've liked to have been, to have the things I'd have liked to have had. I didn't want a child for the sake of that child's life; I wanted her only to replace the child I had never been."

"Pretty deep," he said, feeling uneasy, as if her openness were about to force him to expose his own innermost thoughts, the ones he had found filling his mind during his long days and nights of solitude as he sailed alone across the world's oceans. He wondered if, like Jacquie, once he got them all sorted out, he'd like himself a lot better.

"You're what, thirty years old?" he asked. "If you're going to find someone, you'd better start looking. Why not Eric? A man in his fifties is perfectly capable of fathering children."

She sighed and got to her feet, then sat lightly on the arm of a chair several feet away. "Because I can never love Eric as anything but a father—my father—not the father of my child."

Now why, Ren wondered, did her words give him such satisfaction? It was none of his affair. "You wanted me to be the father of your child, and you didn't love me," he reminded her.

"That was different."

"How?"

Biting her lip, she tried to find ways to explain how it was different, but the words just wouldn't come. Because, she realized, even if she hadn't loved him in the very beginning, she'd soon learned to. So, with his "duty" done, and him none the wiser, she had sent him on his way, before it became impossible for her to let him go.

She slipped from the arm of the chair and crouched to open the damper on the stove, unhook the door, and add another two chunks of wood. The firelight played over her face, gilding it, highlighting her cheekbones, dancing in the aqua eyes she cast toward him. "Like I said, it was a business arrangement."

He pulled her to her feet, holding her in a loose embrace. "Was that all it was?" Inside him desire tightened his muscles again. She smelled so good—sweet, warm, so womanly.

His words, his intense look, the timbre of his voice, reminded her that it had become considerably more than just a business arrangement, regardless of how it had started out. Those first, tentative, awkward moments of embarrassment at finding herself in bed with a stranger—even a stranger whose name she bore—had been terrible. But then he touched her, and something incredible had leaped between them. She had seen her own surprise reflected in his eyes.

Now, suddenly, it was there between them again like an electric current linking them far more tightly than his arms on her waist, or her hands on his elbows. She remembered as well as he did the magic they had found together. She had tried over and over to wipe it from her mind, convince herself it had never happened, but it had a habit of sneaking up on her unawares, kicking her feet out from under her, leaving her weak and breathless and wondering if she would ever, even once before she died, feel those sensations again.

His voice was a deep rumble when he spoke. "For two years, Jacqueline, I've thought of what I found with you. Relived it a hundred times. It became the standard by which other—encounters—would be judged."

Should he tell her how few "encounters" there had been?

He drew in a breath, then exhaled sharply. She felt the warmth of it on her cheek.

"Nothing ever came close. I think, more than anything, that's why I came here, why I went to the trouble of tracking you down. Oh, I could have phoned you, written. Yet I found myself driving hundreds of miles into the back of nowhere in search of you. In search of the magic we'd shared. Is it still there, Jac? Why don't we find out?"

She could feel the heat of his body as he drew her inches closer, the tips of her breasts nearly touching his chest, but not quite. The last small move he was leaving up to her. Did she dare? She wanted desperately to be close to him. She trembled, lifted a hand, and touched the back of his neck with icy fingers. She slid her hand flat against the heat of his skin, took a quarter step closer, and then, with a whispered word of negation, she stepped back out of his reach.

"Hey," he said softly. "Come on Jac."

"I think not," she said, her face taking on a shuttered look she had mastered well, a look that told him, No Trespassing.

Frustration, disappointment, anger, they all surged up in him, and he lifted a hand as if to pull her back into his embrace. To his dismay, she flinched and backed farther from him as if he posed a physical threat.

With a grimace, he dropped his hand. "Don't worry. I've never forced a woman in my life, nor seduced one who was as scared as you are." When she still made no reply, he asked, "Jac, that was why you sent me away, wasn't it?"

At once, she was defensive. Dammit, she had to stop reacting to the man!

"If I hadn't sent you away, you would have left soon enough—willingly, remember? You had what you wanted: your grandfather's money. Speaking of which, I didn't need any of the money you left for me. It's still in the account we opened. I'll sign it back to you."

"I'm not interested in the money," he said impatiently. "I'm interested in finding out what there is about me that scares you so badly."

She laughed. "What a typically male thing to say! Can't a woman simply say no without the man having to define her motives? Can't—"

"Dammit," he interrupted, "I want to know where I went wrong! So will you, just to satisfy my curiosity, tell me why you suddenly began to hate me after all those weeks when we gave each other such pleasure!"

She drew in several deep, calming breaths before she answered. "I didn't hate you." She had the manner of a patient teacher with a stupid pupil. "I don't hate anyone."

Somehow, he knew that what she said was true. When it came right down to it, though, he really knew very little about Jacqueline Train—in spite of the six weeks they'd spent together. But he did know that she didn't hate people. Hate was too closely akin to love.

"It scared you, didn't it, the emotion, the loss of control?" he asked. "Well, let me tell you, Jacqueline, it scared me, too, but I didn't want to run away from it. I wanted to feel it again, and again, and again."

"Are you saying you'd have been willing to give up your great adventure to stay with me just because we were sexually compatible?" she asked icily.

"No! What I'm talking about is what happened the week before I left, when you denied me completely. Dammit, for two years I've thought about it, wondered why you turned so cold so suddenly. I wanted you to thaw once more, Jacqueline. Just once more."

She gazed at him, wondering how he could *not* know how total her "thaw" had been, that in denying him she had denied herself even more, that in suggesting he leave when she did, she was only trying to save herself more heartbreak. "Get out of the situation before the situation gets you," she'd told herself. As a philosophy for life, it left a lot to be desired, she knew. It was a coward's way, but it was the only way she'd been able to handle what was happening to her. She would have lost him anyway. Why not sooner than later? Why not before he began to mean even more to her than he already did? Only it had been too late, of course, far, far too late. It had been too late from the very first day they'd met.

"That was all I wanted from you," he said again. "Just one more night of magic. I wanted you so bad I could taste it."

"A farewell performance?"

He looked at her bleakly. Was she laughing at him? Her face was expressionless. Her voice had been uninflected. He had no way of knowing how she felt, and it made him furious. "That's a lousy thing to call it," he said. "But since that's what you choose to call it, and since I didn't get it, how about a welcome-home performance?"

He pulled her tightly against him and pressed his lips to hers with a desperate kind of tenderness, a growl of frustration rumbling in his throat when she resisted passively, refusing to open her mouth to him. When he grew more insistent, she tossed her head to escape his kiss.

Moving was her biggest mistake. She knew it at once, but the sensation of his mouth stroking over her face was too sweet, and her movements became slower and slower, more and more sensuous, and they both knew she no more wanted out of that embrace than he did. He kissed her temples, her cheeks, her chin. His hands tangled in her hair, sliding through the strands, the pads of his fingers massaging her scalp and the nape of her neck in a slow dance that set her blood aflame. She nearly collapsed, her head falling back to expose the soft flesh of her throat to his seductive kisses.

She realized how she was responding to him, and angrily tried to thrust him away, knowing that her strength was all but gone, but needing to show him that he couldn't win every time—only he could. She wanted him! Lord, how she wanted him. She yearned to absorb his hardness with her softness, to take him into her, to enfold him with her flesh, to tumble with him to the couch and let her senses have full rein over her actions.

He smelled so good. His hair was crisp and springy under her palms. The muscles in his shoulder were quivering as he tilted her head back against it and covered her mouth hotly with his own. She stroked the roughness of his cheek eagerly, feeling his evening beard under her hand, feeling the bones of his face under his skin. If she were a sculptor, she would carve him out of the hardest jade, because only jade would suit the perfection of his structure. His shoulder curved to cradle her as her hands splayed over his back. His thigh, hard and solid, slid between hers, as he rocked her sensitive center against him.

"Ren . . ." She heard the soft gasp arise from her throat and knew he felt it with his lips.

He answered it with a deep sound that might have been her name as he ran the tip of a finger around and around one of her ears, then he slid his leg from between hers. He lifted his head and stared at her, bemused.

"Did I hurt you?" he asked, easing his hold but not letting her go. When she shook her head, her dark curls danced in the lamplight and he never wanted to stop looking into her aqua eyes, which were alive and sparkling. Her cheeks were flushed pink and her breathing was rapid, as ragged as his own.

"Damn," he said, "but you turn me on like no one else ever has. Whatever it is we had before, it's still there for me. Even when you're being bitchy, I want you. Maybe even more then, but I never want to hurt you. I promise, I won't."

You will, you will, she wanted to tell him, but couldn't speak.

He took little nibbling bites of her swollen lips. "You have the most incredible flavor, Jac," he murmured. "I love to kiss you. I want to, but I won't unless you want it just as much."

He might have been asking. He might have been telling. She was incapable of knowing for sure. She didn't want to think. She only wanted to feel. She had gone too long without feeling.

Ren's finger continued to outline her delicate ear, caressing it, tracing its shape from soft lobe to slightly peaked tip. He smiled. "You have ears like an elf. They're pointed. Do you have elves and leprechauns and fairies in your background, Jacqueline Train?"

She squeezed her eyes shut. If he knew, would

he be doing this? If he knew, would he still want her?

"Can you read minds as well as make magic and fly? I didn't know until this morning that you could fly. Do you know what a beautiful picture you made, soaring through the air?"

His fingers trailed down her neck and around the top of her leisure suit, making her shiver. One thumb, rope-hardened and rough, stroked along her jaw line, his other hand moved from her hair to her nape and downward, kneading and massaging as it tracked the valley of her spine.

This tenderness was something she had longed for—to be touched, to be stroked, to be held. Did it matter that he didn't know? He was here for now, not forever. She and Renny had never thought in terms of forever. They never would. But oh, how she wanted to enjoy "now"! She sighed, lifting her face to his.

"Ren . . ."

"Hmm?"

"I like you to touch me. I need you to."

"Like this?" He cupped a hand around one of her breasts, palming the nipple into hardness. His other hand splayed over her buttocks, curving under one side, lifting her up to him, moving her against the shaft of his manhood. She sobbed softly with pleasure, feeling hot and weak and liquid inside.

He was watching her face, looking into her eyes, and knew her passion was growing, keeping pace with his.

"Kiss me, Ren," she whispered.

He covered her lips with his, softly, so softly. He parted them gently with his tongue and teasingly stroked over the lower one, filling her with delight. She wanted that kiss to go on forever.

She would have been content to spend the rest of her natural life with her mouth fused to Renny's. It was beautiful, and she felt warm and safe and fulfilled. When he tried to move back from her, she clung to him and flicked out with her own tongue, seeking deeper contact. The need for far more than just a kiss came rushing over her in heady waves.

At once he met her need, plunging into the hot darkness of her mouth, stroking her tongue with his, holding her body closer, feeling his desire rise with every second. She tilted her head back and spoke his name softly, questioningly.

"Yes," he breathed against her lips. "Oh, yes, Jacquie. More. Give me more."

And she did. She fitted herself to the contours of his body, tangled her hands in his hair, arched her back to fit her breast into his cradling hand, and sobbed again when his thumb began stroking its rigid peak. He answered her soft sounds of pleasure with some of his own, walking her backward to the couch and easing her down.

She felt the wonderful weight of him against her, and let her hands weave their way through his hair, then over his nape and across his shoulders. His back was burning hot when she slid her hands under his sweater, and he shifted sideways just enough that he could push her sweater out of the way. At the sensation of his hand on her bare flesh, she gasped his name. Her bra came undone easily and he took a nipple between thumb and forefinger, squeezing it gently, then holding her entire breast in his hand, as he let his palm roll the aching nipple around and around. She felt her legs part, felt his hardness and power as he settled into the cradle she had provided. In moments she was going to burst into flames, and she wondered dimly if their clothing would disintegrate, wished it would. Her tongue continued to stroke his, the magic growing stronger and stronger, her need growing more powerful, and then, suddenly, unbelievably, totally unexpectedly, there was—*nothing*.

Four

They both tried to pretend. She longed to recapture what she had lost. He continued to caress her and kiss her and whisper to her encouragingly, but they knew it was useless. What she had been feeling, the level of passion as powerful and intense as it had been, was now gone.

With a sigh, he slid his hand from under her clothing, pulling the top of the leisure suit down to meet the waistband of the pants. He lifted his head, looking down into her eyes questioningly. "Jac? What happened?" He knelt on the floor at her side, touching her hair with one hand, gently, soothingly.

There was no censure in his gravelly tone, only caring. How had he known, anyway? she wondered. She had tried not to show it, to go on participating fully, but of course, sensitive, knowledgeable Renny had been aware of her sudden lack of feeling.

"I don't know, Renny," she said, her husky voice unsteady. "I'm sorry." She had wanted that kiss, and more. The desire still lay latent inside her. She ached for his touch, but something in her had rejected it.

She sat up, huddling away from him on one end of the couch. "I didn't mean for us to go that far in the first place, but when we did, I didn't want to stop. I didn't expect to. I'm not a tease, Ren."

"I know," he acknowledged. "But something sure cooled you off. That's never happened to me before."

She shot him a glance. A flash of anger crackled unexpectedly through her.

"May I point out that it didn't happen to you? It happened to me! And maybe it wasn't really there to begin with," she said in a desperate attempt at an explanation. "Maybe it was just sort of an echo of the past, having about as much substance as most echoes."

He laughed with little humor and moved up to sit beside her. "That, my friend, was most definitely no echo."

"I'm not your friend."

He raised one brow. "Would you rather be my wife? I'm surprised. I thought you had more use for friends than husbands."

"Why do you have to be either?"

He frowned and gave her question more consideration than she had thought it warranted. "I don't know, Jac. But something tells me I'm going to have to stay here long enough to find out which I'm going to be."

"You're not staying," she said determinedly, panic bringing her to her feet. "In fact, you're leaving. Now."

He crossed his ankles and linked his hands behind his head, a man fully intending to stay where he sat.

"Ren, dammit, I'm tired. I get up before dawn every morning. You have to go. I really hate to be rude, but you can't stay here. There's a nice little motel in Marsden—the Creekside. You'll be comfortable there." She walked toward the door and back again, adding, "And be careful driving down the mountain. It's a long, slippery drive at night. We don't need any bad publicity this close to opening day."

He sat up. "Just like that? Go, Ren? Leave? Get out? Don't clutter up Jacquie's mountain with your battered body? Wow, you don't mess around, do you, lady?"

His tone may have been joking, but Jacquie knew his feelings were hurt. "Ren, I'm sorry. I'd ask you to stay, but like I said earlier, the hotel—the resort, isn't open."

"Right. And when you do open, you're fully booked because of Thanksgiving. Do you have any objection to my spending the night in the parking lot?"

He sounded bitter, she thought, and wished she

knew how she could let him stay and still be safe herself.

"I have a sleeping bag in my Blazer," he went on when she made a helpless little gesture. "And I got up a long time before dawn this morning. I'm just as tired, if not more tired, than you are. I'd rather not risk the long, steep drive down an unfamiliar road. My life is pretty important to me, and I try not to risk it unnecessarily." Dammit, he was not leaving. If he could stay the night, then he'd be in a good position to take up their problems with her again tomorrow.

"Hah! Coming from the guy who just completed a single-handed jaunt around the world in a thirty-foot sloop, that's pretty hard to believe." Damn, but he could make her feel churlish without really trying! she realized. She gave in. "All right. I guess you can stay in your car. We don't allow camping, but what can they say? After all, you are my husband."

He grinned with little mirth. "What can they say? Oh, lots. *Resort Manager's Husband Freezes to Death in Parking Lot on Night of Return from High Seas. No Room at the Inn.* Neat headline, huh? Great publicity before opening day."

He shrugged into his jacket, pulled on his boots, and opened the door. "Well, night, Jac. See you," he said, and sauntered slowly away, kicking up little puffs of snow as he went, his hands stuffed deeply into his pockets.

Didn't he even have gloves? she wondered. Or a hat? Was his sleeping bag warm enough for the icy mountain conditions? Oh, why had he come back to plague her?

She shuddered at the thought of the headline he'd so kindly composed for her imagination to work on. Great publicity, just what she needed. The captain would kill her—or worse, he'd fire her for showing lousy judgment. She sighed a gusty, angry sigh and tugged on her heavy jacket before stuffing her feet into her boots.

Damn the man! Why couldn't he have found a nice little South Pacific island and gone native? She didn't need this aggravation. She didn't need headlines, or problems, or him. Oh, yeah? her conscience reminded her. Headlines or problems, maybe, but him? Him she needed, but it was a need she meant to fight to the death. Only she knew she wouldn't sleep if she had to think of him spending the night huddled in an ill-equipped vehicle, risking death by hypothermia—and she also knew that her feelings had nothing whatever to do with headlines.

"There's a spare room in my chalet," she said grudgingly when he opened the door she hammered on. "You may as well spend the night there."

His soft laugh puffed a cloud out in the air between them as he said, "Thanks, Jac. I appreciate it."

"But bring your sleeping bag. The bed's not made up. And make no mistake. This is not an invitation for you to share *my* bed!"

With a solemn nod, he carefully gathered up his sleeping bag. Facing her in the stinging cold outside the dubious shelter of his car, he said, "I'll share your bed when you invite me into it graciously, Jacqueline, not when you try to challenge me by being bitchy to force my way into it."

Was that what she'd been doing? she wondered as she crawled under the luxurious warmth of her goose down comforter. She wanted to cry, but she didn't cry easily. She wanted to sleep, but was wide awake. She wanted to go downstairs and climb in beside Renny and succumb to the aching need that was filling her, body and soul, heart and mind. He disturbed her badly, and she didn't know what to do about it except send him away. She had done it once, and she could do it again.

Tomorrow.

"Jacqueline, are you aware of exactly who it is you are married to?"

She laughed. "Eric! Of course I am. What kind of a question is that, for heaven's sake?"

"But you never told me." He reached over and knocked the contents of his pipe into the ashtray she kept in her office for his personal use. No one else was permitted to smoke there. "*The Renegade!*" he exclaimed. "Hell, Jac, if I'd known, I wouldn't have worried about your being all alone in the world. Lordy, lordy, the Renegade Knight!"

Jacquie blinked. The Renegade Knight? She supposed it was appropriate, but she'd never heard it before. "What—"

"I've given him a job, of course," Eric went on. "It was the only way I could keep him here. He's got this weird idea that if he doesn't work, he can't stay. I admire him, of course. No man worthy of the name Renegade would want his wife to support him, but hell, Renny Knight could write his own ticket on any ski slope in the world. Hiring him just to sit in the lounge and talk to the guests would be worth it, but he's actually willing to give lessons. I've made him chief instructor."

Jacquie shot to her feet, hands on hips. "Eric, would you please tell me what you're talking about? Hired him? You have all the instructors you need!" Oh, damn, damn! If Eric had hired Ren, there was nothing she could do about it. The ski school came under Eric's jurisdiction.

But wait, she thought. Accommodations came under hers. She placed her knuckles on her desk, leaned forward, and looked Eric straight in the eye, saying slowly and clearly, "Renny Knight is not staying on this mountain."

"Oh-oh." Eric frowned. "What's the matter, honey? You're not scared of him, are you? He hasn't—"

"I am not scared of anybody!" she said aggressively. "I . . . well, I thought you had a full staff. I'd hate to think you hired Renny because he's my husband. I don't like nepotism."

"Honey, I hired him because I'd have been a fool to let him go. But wouldn't he belong here even if he wasn't the Renegade Knight? You're here, aren't you? Now that he's home, where else would he stay?"

Jacquie didn't know but thought an oilfield in Kuwait might be nice. She whirled around and stalked away, staring out the plate-glass window at the slopes where several skiers dipped and glided like colorful, tropical fish swirling in an ocean of white. Among them, she realized, was one who stood a good head taller than all the rest. Renny Knight—surrounded by admiring women. Inside her something flipped over, leaving her feeling hollow. "Dammit, Eric, what have you done?"

"Don't swear at me, Jacqueline! I should be cussing at you. I thought you called him Ben, not Ren, when you told me about him. How could you let *Renny Knight* go away and waste his time sailing for two years? He belongs to the slopes, to the world of winter sports. Hell, not only was he on the national ski team, taking two gold medals on the World Cup circuit, he won the Mountain Man Winter Triathlon three years running. His time in all three remains unbeaten.

"The first time he entered the snowshoe section he simply galloped up the mountainside with those long, sleek strides of his and left the others behind—and he didn't even use ski poles. The man's strength is unbelievable. And his endurance!"

Oh, sure, she thought. She certainly did know

all about his endurance! But Eric would not want to hear about that. No, most definitely Eric wouldn't want to hear about that. She'd be a lot better off, too, if she quit thinking about it, about him. Only how could she, when Eric seemed to have a compulsive need to talk about Renny Knight—and she had a compulsive desire to listen.

"Do you know how hard it is to run up a mountain wearing bearpaw snowshoes, and then go directly into the cross-country ski run?" he demanded, not waiting for a reply. It was just as well, since she didn't have a reply to give him. "He skied along behind the leader until the last two miles, then whipped past and finished a good fifteen seconds ahead. And at the end of the speed-skating ordeal, he'd opened that gap to three full minutes. It was his first time in the triathlon, Jacqueline! He entered three more times and in each one he did better and better. Then he quit. No one knew where he had gone, or why he left his record undefended. Some said he'd married and his wife told him to quit."

Eric's recital drew to a halt as he stared, horrified, at Jacquie. "You? You did that?"

"Me? No. Of course not. I didn't even know he—" She shut her mouth, returned to her high-backed swivel chair, and sat down behind her desk. In San Diego skiing wasn't something she thought about or heard about. There it was Ren's prowess as a sailor that was discussed—and his prowess as a lover.

Eric went on. "Another rumor had it that he'd

crashed in a downhill ski run and was a vegetable, and yet another had him wiped out on drugs." He shook his head wonderingly. "And none of that was true. He was off playing Robinson Crusoe. What a guy, Jacqueline! What a guy!"

Sentiments she could only echo, even if she did it silently. The sooner the man was off the mountain and out of her life the better.

Eric reached into his shirt pocket for his pouch and filled his pipe, puffing hard as he held a match to the tobacco, eyeing Jacquie through the resulting cloud of smoke. "You know, honey, it's a good thing you were already married to him when I asked you. Because I'd have had to let you out of it some way or another if you'd become my wife. Renny Knight is the right man for you. If I'd searched the world over, I couldn't have picked a better man for you myself. You treat him right, sweetheart. You hang on to him, and if you're having a little difference of opinion, well, try to get over it."

Jacquie could only stare at her dearest, oldest friend. How could she tell him she meant nothing to Renny? After having told Eric she adored her absent husband, how could she now come up with a story to suit the facts as they really were? How could she make it clear to Eric that Renny couldn't go on working at Roseate Mountain? And if he did stay, she'd cause gossip and rumors by making her husband take a room in the staff quarters or, even worse, in the motel in Marsden?

She knew for sure that Renny was not spending

one more night in her house if she could help it. The trouble was, she knew perfectly well that she wasn't going to be able to help it. That being the case, how was she going to help herself keep him out of her bed?

Thanksgiving arrived and with it a happy influx of guests, and Jacquie was too busy to brood. Well, she was too busy to brood much. She worked hard every day, mixing, mingling, keeping an eye and an ear to each aspect of management, leaving her massive paperwork for the evenings. She told herself it wasn't solely because of Renny that she worked late every night. She'd often stayed at the office late, alone with no distractions.

Yet as the days passed, she found herself leaving the office earlier and earlier, and returning there after dinner less and less. Even if they didn't talk, if he sketched—sketches he carefully did not share with her—and she did crossword puzzles, or they just sat and read or watched movies on the VCR, or did a jigsaw puzzle together, it was nice having him there. It was nice in the morning, too, as he was always up first and had the coffee made, the fire lit, the house warm for her before she came downstairs.

She could, she knew, get used to that kind of pampering.

He was so darn . . . nice, she thought now, sitting across from him as they turned over the pieces of a new jigsaw he'd bought in Marsden.

She hadn't had to fight him off, and knew she was disappointed. Where were the kisses she had expected him to sneak? The passes his actions on that first day had warned her to expect? The sexy innuendos she thought she'd dreaded? They simply didn't exist—because he simply didn't want her? Was that a fair assumption?

She knew it wasn't, and, above all, Jacquie liked to be fair. He'd told her once, and he probably didn't think he had to say it again: When she invited him into her bed graciously, then he'd be glad to accept.

But she didn't quite have the courage. She methodically turned puzzle pieces right side up, thinking of the time a few days before when she had come home early, cooked dinner for the two of them, lit a candle, and played soft music. How gracious did she have to get? Was she supposed to come right out and ask?

She sighed softly. She knew, still being scrupulously fair, that when she was completely ready, if ever, she wouldn't hesitate to come right out and say it. It would be nice, though, she thought, if he'd try to sweep her off her feet. Damn! She had been making her own decisions for nearly half her life. Now she wanted one of the most important ones taken from her as if she were some kind of weak-minded idiot? If that were the case, she was doomed to disappointment.

Right after the intimate dinner she'd prepared, he'd gone out—to a poker game. Sure, she thought, wondering if his poker partner was the bouncy redhead from the ski shop or the skinny—anorexic maybe—brunette guest who'd been Renny's dancing partner for most of one evening. Oh, he'd frequently asked Jacquie to dance, and she'd accepted once. It had been a slow dance, and being close to him, breathing in his scent, feeling the heat of his hands on her, the strength of his muscles under her palms had made her feel giddy and stupid and weak. It had made her want, as never before, for him to take the decision out of her hands, to make it all by himself, to overwhelm her with kisses and caresses and the passion that could whip through them both so quickly. Wildfire loving, that was what she wanted. She sighed again.

"What's the matter?" he asked, smiling across the table at her.

"Nothing." She was an idiot. She should be grateful that he wasn't rushing her.

"You sigh twice in two minutes and then say there's nothing wrong? Is there something you'd like to talk about, Jac?"

She wondered what he'd say if she told him the truth, that she'd like to walk up those stairs hand in hand with him, slide down into the warmth of her bed, and make slow, sweet love with him all night long. She tingled at the thought. She wanted him, all right, but she worried about what would happen if they started something and she suffered the same kind of failure she'd experienced the night he came back. No, it was better to leave him to the skinny brunettes and the bubbly redheads of the world. They could handle their feelings a lot better than she could.

For a long moment he watched the play of expressions across her face, wondering what she was thinking, but when she shook her head and murmured that she didn't have anything in particular on her mind, he returned his attention to the puzzle.

When he finally looked up again, he said, "Do you always do that? Start with the border and then work toward the center?"

She set another piece in and nodded, smiling at his quizzical expression. "Sure. I like to have a frame of reference."

"Restrictions," he said, frowning.

"No, not really. Perimeters, maybe. They're necessary. How can I know what form the picture is going to take if I don't know its boundaries? I couldn't work the way you do, a bit of this, a bit of that, nothing . . . connected, no structure. Look, you have a little of the tower built, and some of the bridge, half a tree." She took the lid of the box he'd leaned against the base of a lamp and turned it face down so he couldn't see it. "How do you know what goes where now?"

"Do I have to know? Can't I just take each piece as it comes and trust that the whole picture will fall together eventually?"

"Sure," she said easily. "I suppose you can, but I can't. I need to know where things are, how they'll affect other things I do and be affected by my actions. For instance, if I put this corner piece here, it links up the bottom and the left side. Oh, rats, it doesn't. Must be the sky, not the reflection of sky." She searched through the loose pieces in vain. "Well, you know what I mean. Things need to be linked, connected, not jumbled and haphazard, then they can form a complete picture. I like to do it methodically."

"I can see that." He handed her the correct corner piece and watched, smiling, as she clicked it into place and patted it with satisfaction.

"I've seen you do crosswords too," he said several moments later. "Do you like all kinds of puzzles?"

She nodded. "Eric started me on jigsaws when I had measles. I wasn't allowed to read, but nobody seemed to think jigsaws would bother my eyes."

"Where did you meet Eric?"

She hesitated, and he sensed that he was in danger of receiving her No Trespassing look, but she bit her lip and said tersely, "Back East."

"You grew up back there?"

She nodded. "Give me some more of that pale blue, will you? It's sky, and you're hogging it. It goes in this corner I'm working on."

He slid a pile of pieces over to her and then covered her hand with his before she could pull it away. "Hey, I'm not just being nosey, Jac. I like you. I want to get to know you better. Tell me how you met Eric."

"It . . . was a long time ago. I don't remember much about it. He was my friend, that's all. Did you ever notice how much he looks like George C. Scott?"

Renny nodded and smiled. "And did you ever notice how much he tries to emphasize that resemblance in the way he dresses, walks, and talks?"

Jacquie laughed softly. "Yeah. I noticed." It was nice to have Ren to share things with. It wasn't an observation any of her employees—or Eric's—would have shared with her. She wished she could open up more with Ren, talk to him the way he wanted her to. But the habit of not talking was so ingrained, the reasons so firmly entrenched in her mind, that she doubted she would ever be able to do it easily.

And it didn't matter anyway; he wouldn't be staying. Renny Knight never stayed anywhere for long.

She pulled her hand out from under his and got to her feet. "I'm going up to bed now, Ren. Good night."

He stood and for a moment looked at her. What would she do if he stepped right over the coffee table and hauled her into his arms? He ached to do it. Every time he looked at her, his body tightened with need, with the desire to break through the barriers she kept between them.

He merely reached out and stroked her hair back from her forehead in a quiet, almost brotherly caress, and said, "Sure. Good night, Jac," and once more watched her walk up the stairs.

He considered storming up there after her, forcing a confrontation that he was ninety-nine percent sure would end up with him lying in her bed, which he had never seen but which figured largely in his fantasies. He clenched his teeth and balled his fists at his sides.

Patience. It had never been one of his stronger suits, and though he had learned to exercise it somewhat out on the ocean alone, he was no longer alone, he no longer wanted to be alone, and his patience was wearing very, very thin.

Five

Ren lay in the narrow bed in the room below Jacquie's, thinking, as he did so often, about her. Right now, his mind dwelt on the previous Saturday night and the torture he'd gone through watching her dance with other men, some of them guests, some staff, and how he'd wanted to break heads and faces and maybe a few legs and arms. Violence had never been a part of his nature—until now. He'd enjoyed the company of women, and if they chose to dance with someone else, why, that was fine. He could do the same. In fact, he'd done so on Saturday night, but it hadn't helped. The only one he wanted to dance with was Jacqueline, and she had danced with him only once—stiffly, clearly not enjoying either the dance or his company, and was just as clearly relieved when he let her go. And he had let her go with reluctance.

What was going on anyway? What was going on with him? Jacqueline Train was just another woman, dammit. There was no need for him to get tied up in knots over her. He had enjoyed her company during their six weeks together, but most of that enjoyment had been sexual. That part of their relationship had been fantastic, and if he had his way, they'd be enjoying themselves now.

He wasn't getting his own way, however, so why did he hang around?

He'd never thought he could—or would want to—have a relationship with any woman that did not include sex. Yet he did with Jacquie. He had to admit he liked her. He liked being with her, wanted more and more of her company, but she continued her elusive ways and there was little he could do about it except be patient. He sighed. Patience was a new and unwieldy characteristic for him, and he couldn't quite get a grip on why something in him demanded he continue to practice it—but something did. Something told him that waiting would pay off in the end.

In the end, it was the exhaustion caused by hard physical work in the outdoors at a high altitude that saved him. He slept, but each time he awoke he was intensely aware of Jacquie in bed in the room over his—except for the nights when he awoke to hear her creeping down the stairs and slipping outside.

Thoughts about where she could be going preyed on his mind unmercifully and kept him awake until she returned, then long after she had gone back to bed. Where did she go? To see whom?

That night, as he had for the previous two nights, he heard her go out. Again he waited for her to come back, and as on each of the other nights, the wait grew more and more interminable, his imagination more and more vivid, the pictures his mind drew, more and more graphic. In the morning he was a wreck.

"What's the matter?" Eric asked.

Renny barked a smart reply back at him. Could it be Eric? he wondered. In spite of what she'd said about her feelings for Eric, could it be him?

Elsie, his good friend and constant source of treats and information, noticed his foul mood, too, and offered him lemon meringue pie, brownies, and her special, extra delicious concoction called butter tarts, trying to perk up his appetite. Elsie surely knew, he decided. Elsie knew everything about everybody on the mountain and about most of the people in Marsden where she lived. Why didn't she tell him? Didn't he have the right to know where his wife went at night?

Why didn't he simply ask Jacqueline? he asked himself.

Renny rolled over in bed, coughed, heard her feet hit the floor softly over his head for the fourth night running, and groaned. He hadn't asked Jacqueline where she went for the very same reason that he hadn't asked Jacqueline much of anything: It was too damned hard to get an answer out of her, and he was too damned scared of being told to get out—out of her house, and out of her life. He wasn't ready to do either yet, not until she came to him, not until he'd had enough of her, had tired of her. Then, maybe, he'd be able to go on to something else, someone else. But where? And who? He couldn't visualize any other place for him—or any other woman. Oh, hell, the whole thing was nuts.

Jacquie turned over again. This time, it was her shoulder that hurt. There was a wrinkle in her sheet. She sat up, smoothed out the wrinkle, lay back down, listened. Renny rolled over in his sleep. She heard his bed creak. In a few minutes, he'd cough, or mumble—or snore. There was no point in her trying to sleep. Again insomnia was keeping her eyes wide open and gritty. Renny . . . asleep . . . downstairs. The knowledge filled her with longing. Every night it grew worse, and every night there was only one thing she knew to do about it: get out of the house.

She had to get up and go to the pool, but she feared that at this rate people might notice her ski tracks even though the trail started behind her chalet, out of sight. The pool was hers, and she guarded it jealously.

But risk or not, the pool was what she needed tonight. Again.

Silently she arose, and just as silently she dressed. The stairs squeaked, but she kept moving. Little whispers of sound wouldn't disturb

Renny. She remembered how soundly he slept. During their six weeks together she had often thought that the depth of his sleep bordered on the pathological. A sad smile curved her mouth. She also remembered that when he awoke, he was always fully awake, ready for whatever was going on.

She was trying not to think about the past, but oh, how hard it was not to! If only she could forget how much she wanted him. As each day went by, she needed him more and more, and she knew it was her own fault that she was still sleeping alone. Could she have another short-term affair with him? Because he was going to leave for sure.

Maybe if she hadn't found his sketches she wouldn't feel so certain that it was only a matter of time before he was gone again. She shouldn't have looked at them, but Renny, who was normally neat, had left his sketches in a pile on the kitchen table, and she had looked. The first few had been nothing but incomprehensible lines, angles, and curves labeled with his incredibly precise printing, all to do with stress and wave action. It had taken several pages before she realized exactly what it was she was seeing, and then, she knew he planned to leave.

The memory of what she had gone through when he'd left before was constantly with her. Could she go through that again?

She put on her boots, her jacket, hat, and mitts and eased the door open without turning on a light. Her cross-country skis were by the door, and she stepped into the bindings as she steadied herself with her poles, then slid toward the back of the chalet.

Everything was still. Everyone but she slept. As she slipped into the forest, skiing along between black trees, feeling the tingle of the air on her face, feeling her taut muscles stretch and loosen, she picked up her speed, listening to the *sisss, sisss, sisss* of her skis, and realized that somewhere above the canopy of trees a moon was shining.

It was only a sickle of a moon she saw, coming out into the clearing by the pool, but the light it cast reflected off the snow, providing enough illumination to make the ethereal streams of mist rising from the pool, which she had dubbed the ghost dancers, seem to twist and flutter as if beckoning her seductively into their midst.

Quickly shedding her skis and jamming them into the snow, she jumped down onto a flat rock at the edge of the steam cloud, becoming one with the ghost dancers, inhaling their warm tangy scent, feeling them soft against her face.

No snow lay here, no ice. The rock was warm to the touch as she peeled off her clothes and left them heaped on top of her boots next to her towel.

Stepping into the water was like coming home. Slightly warmer than her normal bath, it bubbled and tingled around her; she thought the effervescence might come from the minerals in the water, but it might just as well have been caused by pressure within the earth's crust that had forced it to the surface.

As hot springs went, it was a baby. The pool itself was only ten feet across at its widest and was less than twice that long. It came frothing out from behind the rock she now reclined on, moved over her body, and swirled in eddies past her toes, then disappeared again into another fissure. To her knowledge, it was a new spring, brought forth by a minor quake the area had experienced the first winter of her tenure. She had discovered it a couple of months after she had found the glade in which it lay. The first snowfall had tempted her to don cross-country gear and explore her new domain, and at that time there had been no spring in the tiny, perfect glade. Still, she had liked the area and had returned often to its solitude and beauty. Then the quake had come. It had done no damage, simply rattled a few windows. It had been a topic of conversation for the rest of the day, and then had been forgotten—by everyone but Jacqueline. She was sure the quake had been responsible for the bit of heaven where she now lay.

She smiled, remembering how startled she had been to find warm mineral water filling the lower level of her personal glade. She hadn't intended to keep it a secret for more than a few days. It was just, she decided, that she wanted a chance to enjoy it alone for a while. But that "while" had stretched and stretched, and she took guilty pleasure in maintaining her secret.

A shadow crossed the moon, and her gaze followed the path of an owl in flight. It swooped, rose up several feet from the snow, and soared aloft again, clearly having missed its target. She was glad.

Then, through the mist, she thought she saw another shadow. She went very still, staring, but the steam thickened at that moment. Rising to a crouch, she peered through it. Then, confident the steam provided a cloaking veil, she stood. When she had a clear patch to see through moments later, she saw nothing, no one. She watched for several more minutes until she was certain of her solitude, but even then didn't return to the water. She dried herself off with the towel she had brought and dressed.

At home the soft sound of Renny's snoring came from behind his closed bedroom door as Jacquie paused before ascending the stairs. She listened for a moment or two, frowned, and then went to bed. The enervation brought on by her long, hot mineral bath took over, and she slept.

"Wow!" Ren came out of his room and stopped in front of Jacquie, gazing down at her while he took her hands and held her arms away from her body, admiring her. She wore a blue dress with a draped bodice and full skirt that outlined her shape faithfully as it swirled around her sheer-nylon-clad legs. Her tiny waist was cinched by a wide silver belt. On her feet she wore a pair of black pumps with three-inch heels. Her dark hair had been brushed until it lay in soft, glistening curls all over her head. Her small ears were adorned with glittering blue stones. All dressed up for the Friday night dinner in the lodge, she was something to behold, Ren decided.

He had an almost overwhelming impulse to kiss each pink-shell ear in turn, but her impenetrable cool manner stopped him.

Oh, Lord, he thought, would he ever be able to forget the vision he had seen the night before? She hadn't looked cool then, wreathed in mist, standing naked and lovely and alert, her head up and tilted to one side as she watched and listened. She had looked right at him. Had she seen him? She'd said nothing, given no indication that she suspected he'd followed her the night before, seen her in her secret place, and then like a coward slipped as silently back into the shadows as he'd come.

Nothing in her attitude now suggested that she knew he had intruded, and he had to suppress the urge to tell her. But, didn't they say confession was good for the soul? Hell! He almost snorted aloud. It wasn't for the sake of his soul he wanted to confess. Once, just once, he wanted to see that impenetrable cool of hers shattered. He wanted to see shock in her eyes—and whatever else might leap into them.

Jacquie looked him over, hiding her desire. He

was magnificent. Tall, straight, his shoulders broad enough for two men, his waist narrow, his hips taut and hard. She could remember the smoothness of his skin, the steel of his muscles, the quiver as he . . .

"You don't look so bad yourself," she said, swallowing hard. She ran her gaze up his dark suit from the front of which peeked a light blue shirt and red and navy striped tie. For a moment her hands itched to follow the path her gaze had taken.

He'd always been a handsome man, but the years had added an element to his looks that she couldn't quite define, she thought, slipping her fingers out of his easy clasp and stepping back, because not only did he look good, he smelled great too. He could have come in from a day in the sun and salt air of the California coast, rather than a day in the fog and snow of an inland mountain town. It made her head swim and made something deep inside her turn to liquid heat. All she had to do was invite him into her bed—"graciously."

After last night, however, would she ever be able to do it? If only she hadn't found his tracks and discovered it had been he she had glimpsed. If only he hadn't pretended to snore when he heard her come home. If only . . .

"Ready to go?" he asked, pulling her out of her fantasy world.

"Oh, yes. Sure. You?"

He shrugged. "Ready as I'll ever be."

"I hope you realize you're getting paid for these

evening appearances," she said. "That should make it easier. I remember how much you hated the socializing your parents tried to impose on you."

"I've found I don't mind this kind of socializing nearly as much." Surprisingly, it was true. Where he had resisted very strongly the social life his parents had tried to force on him, he didn't find the dinner hour in the lodge an onerous duty. There was a delightful lack of formality in the atmosphere and a genuineness in the people Roseate Lodge attracted; they were very different from those in his parents' social circle. Even the gala Thanksgiving dinner two weeks earlier hadn't been hard to bear for him. What had happened the previous Saturday, though, he told himself, was not going to be repeated this evening. If Jacqueline danced, dammit, she was dancing with him—exclusively. That was that, job or no job.

It was part of his job as well as Jacquie's to dress more formally for dinner on weekends. It provided an excuse for the guests to show off their best clothes, since they usually dressed in casual attire during the week. All the department heads were expected to put in frequent appearances in the dining room, but only on weekends was any degree of formality required. As chief ski instructor, he supposed he could be considered a department head, though technically that position was Eric's. A law unto himself, Eric never ate in the dining room. "Your job, son," he'd said, when the subject came up. So Renny wore two hats on the evenings he spent in the dining room;

when he was with Jacquie, he was her husband. On the days she didn't show up, he was simply the chief ski instructor.

It wasn't part of his job to hold Jacquie's coat as she slipped into it, or to lean close so he could smell her hair. Nor was it his job to steady her as she took off her high heels and donned her boots. Those things he did because he wanted to. Yet wasn't that the same reason he had become a ski instructor? Because of Jacquie? He had to admit he enjoyed his job as he'd never enjoyed another. He got more satisfaction out of seeing a terrified, crouching novice with slippery boards attached to his boots turn into a smiling, proud skier, than he had ever gotten out of designing a row of ticky-tacky little boxes or another look-alike shopping center in another dusty, look-alike town.

"I love the place at this time of night," said Jacquie as they walked across the floodlit expanse of snow toward the lodge, where lights blazed from every window, turned golden by the softly swirling flakes that had been falling steadily since before noon. "It looks so warm, so welcoming."

"If it is, it's because you make it so," he said, taking her hand and swinging their arms between them. "I think you like your job as much as I like mine."

She glanced up at him, startled. "You like your job?" His fingers curled around hers and her entire body reacted. Stop that! she told herself.

"Yes, I like it," he said. "I was just thinking how much more I enjoy this job than any other job I've had. I get up each morning looking forward to the day, eager for my first class to begin. Teaching is something I never thought I'd be good at, but I love it."

"But you insist on working mainly with the adult bunny-hill crowd. How come, Ren? I'd have thought there wouldn't be enough challenge in that for the Renegade."

He wanted to tell her that the biggest challenge of his life was going on right under her nose, and she was too busy managing a hotel to see it, to appreciate it. He shrugged. "I'm not sure why, but maybe it's because they really want lessons. There they stand, six or eight of them in varying degrees of terror, but so determined to master the sport that they'll accept the falls and the humiliation and the fear. And then the first time they come down the slope with any kind of control, you'd think it was all my doing. They look up to me, I guess, think I'm some kind of superhero."

"So adulation has its appeal?" she asked, teasing him.

He was so startled by the warmth in her voice that he let go of her hand and looked down into her beautiful eyes. Determined to make a move, some kind of a move, any kind of a move while she was in a relaxed frame of mind, he slid his arm around her. She stiffened for a moment, and then softened against him. They shared the first real smile they had allowed themselves to smile in days.

"Ren . . ." Her warm breath puffed across his cheek. Her lips were parted, they looked full, inviting, warm. He was going to kiss her—damn the consequences.

"Tell me how you feel about teaching," she said quickly, and he swallowed hard as he forced himself to concentrate on controlling his urges. She had to come to him, dammit. He knew she would, he could sense that the time was near. How many times had he glanced up from sketching his designs to see an expression of hunger in her eyes, a hunger she quickly cloaked. It was there, he knew it. He recognized it as the same hunger that was tearing his gut apart.

"I've . . . never been in charge of anyone before," he said slowly, consideringly, feeling his way through his thoughts. "Never had other people rely on me—and my expertise, I guess you could call it—to help them achieve their goals. I like it. It makes me feel good."

She nodded, blinking as snowflakes stuck to her lashes. He pulled her under the shelter of a large pine tree, leaning back on the trunk out of the falling snow. Looping his hands loosely behind her back, he drew her close enough so that their toes touched. She shook her head to send a shower of gleaming snow off into the night. Her dangling earrings caught the light and played blue fire across her neck and under her chin, and he nearly gave in to the desire to touch those moving sparkles of color with the tip of his tongue. He knew she would taste as good as she smelled.

She stood very still in his loose embrace, her hands in the pockets of her coat, her gaze fully on him, questioning, wary, he thought, and he deliberately tightened the rein on himself, forced his body to be still and his attention to return to their conversation.

"When I teach people to ski, I think I'm doing it as much for myself as I am for them."

"I can understand that," she said, turning her gaze from his toward the warm, glowing windows of the lodge. The door swung open regularly to admit happy people and spill out light and music. Each time it opened, they could see the colored, twinkling lights of the huge Christmas tree in the foyer.

"If, as you say," she went on, "I make people feel warm and welcome, it's because it makes me feel good to do it. I like my job too." She frowned and spoke slowly, diffidently, and it surprised him; he didn't think of Jacquie as diffident. Ordinarily she was very sure of herself—of her ideas and aims and beliefs—if not of her feelings.

"Ren . . . you know, I think sometimes that the guests are secondary to my enjoyment. That's wrong, isn't it? I only want them here because without them, there wouldn't be, couldn't be, a hotel. I love my hotel. I love any hotel."

Curious, he said, "Any hotel? Why's that?"

She bit her lip and looked back at him. Then, almost as much to herself as to him she said, "A hotel never ever locks its doors. I like to know that somewhere in this world there is a door that can never be locked against me."

Suddenly he had to swallow hard against a lump that formed in his throat. He lifted one hand and touched the blue fire reflected on her throat. "What do you mean?" he asked softly and saw her face take on its guarded look, the one he hated more and more.

"Nothing," she said, then laughed, dispelling the mood as she spun out of his reach.

"Dammit, Jac, don't do this to me!" he said, catching her hand and pulling her back against him, pinning her with one arm behind her waist, the other hand at the nape of her neck. "For once you were being candid with me, opening up an inch or two. You were talking about that secret childhood of yours, weren't you? Jac, please," he added.

She shook her head. "I don't talk about my childhood. I told you two years ago all I ever mean to tell you. All anyone needs to know."

"I'm not just anyone, dammit," he said with a growl. "I'm your husband. I think I have a right to know more than the bare fact that your childhood was—how did you put it?—less than ideal, best forgotten. I told you all about my childhood. I'm a blabbermouth. So how come I got mixed up with a clam?"

"Renny, you aren't 'mixed up' with me," she said chidingly. "Please, let me go. We aren't exactly hidden under this tree."

"Why should we hide, Jacquie?"

"I—no reason, I guess."

"And why should you hide your past from me?"

"Renny, I'm not hiding it. I'm just—forgetting it."

"You know something?" he asked, loosening his hold on her. "If you really were capable of forgetting it, you'd be a much happier woman, but you refuse to forget it, don't you? It's with you all the time, coloring everything you think and say and do. Somewhere back there, somebody locked a little girl out, and she's still out. Only trouble is, she's keeping the grown woman locked out there with her."

"Will you quit trying to analyze me, for heaven's sake? What I said was unimportant. My one bit of leftover childhood foolishness. It was more symbolic than real, so let's forget it. Now come on. The Poor Little Match Girl is starving. How about Little Lord Fauntleroy? Do you want to eat, or don't you?"

Six

Renny stood staring after Jacqueline as she strode away toward the lodge.

The Poor Little Match Girl? Little Lord Fauntleroy? Was that how she saw them? Was that her hangup?

He shook his head and loped toward the steps. The idea was preposterous! She knew how he felt about his family, their way of life, their money. He wanted no part of the illustrious San Diego Knights, senior members of the architectural firm of Knight, Knight, and Fisher—Fisher being his equally illustrious brother-in-law, a full member of the family by virtue of having been properly bought and paid for. The firm was now Knight and Fisher, he reminded himself. When he had failed to join the firm, and his grandfather had died, there was only one Knight left. And that was the way it was going to stay.

Jacquie gave him a smile as she took her shoes from him in the foyer and exchanged her boots for them, then slipped her hand through his arm, walking with him, smiling, greeting guests, pausing here and there to chat for a minute, the perfect hostess . . . and also a perfect enigma to her husband.

Later he wondered if it had been a case of not being careful enough in what he wished for—because he just might get it. When it all began, he didn't know exactly what was happening, didn't know that before the night was out things that had been clear to him would be so muddled that he'd doubt they could ever be sorted out.

It started so innocuously too.

"Jacquie?" A man at a table reached out a hand and tentatively touched her arm. "Aren't you Jacquie Jensen?" he asked, getting to his feet.

Tilting her head, she looked at him, trying to place him. Then she smiled warmly. "My goodness! Kevin? What a surprise! You've changed a lot. You must be two feet taller, a hundred pounds heavier, and a whole lot better looking," she said, grinning. "No zits."

"Thanks. It's been a long time, Jac, but you've hardly changed at all. You're certainly no taller, and you probably weigh less. What a small world. All the way from Elephant Mountain to this one?"

His companion cleared her throat gently, and he swung guiltily toward her. "Jacquie, I'd like you to meet my wife, Andrea. Honey, this is Jacqueline—er—Jensen. We were—brother and sister, I guess you could say—way back when. You left when you were what, Jacquie? Thirteen?"

She nodded. "About that. Nice to meet you, Andrea. This is my husband, Renny Knight."

Kevin looked impressed. "Say, are you the Mrs. Knight who runs this place? Congratulations, Jacquie. Really a case of chickens coming home to roost, isn't it? I ended up owning a restaurant in Everett. Guess all that enforced training they put us through paid off after all."

Jacquie nodded, wishing Kevin had never turned up, but since he had, that he would shut up. He was part of a period in her life she preferred not to think about—and never talked about. The only one who knew about it was Eric, and after one discussion of it last year, they had agreed to put it behind them. Not that either of them ever truly could, of course, but he went along with her preference not to discuss it.

She managed to change the subject by asking, "Is this your first visit to Roseate Lodge, Andrea?"

The woman nodded eagerly. "And we love it. Our room is so cosy and quaint with its sloped ceilings and flowery wallpaper. It may be our first visit, but it's not going to be our last. We've booked a chalet for two weeks in January with another couple. They were here last year. They mentioned a Jacquie Knight. Maybe you remember them? The Colliers? Big guy with red hair? She's a tall blonde. From Everett. They're our next-door neighbors."

"Yes. Yes, I do. Ted and Marlene, right? I look forward to seeing them again, and you. I hope you enjoy your weekend. I'll have to ask you to excuse me now. What are you drinking? Let me order you another round. I must see the chef before he serves dinner." Her smile told her guests that Jacqueline knew they, as restauranteurs, would understand perfectly.

Beaming, saying that they would have to get together again to talk about old times, Kevin shook Ren's hand, kissed Jacquie's cheek, and reluctantly let them go.

Her head spinning, her mind filled with a thousand lies she might offer to Renny that would explain Kevin's words, Jacquie wished she could run and hide somewhere.

To her surprise, Ren didn't question her. Instead, he said wonderingly, "How could you possibly remember one couple out of the hundreds who come here every season?"

She drew in a steadying breath and pushed open the swinging doors that led to the kitchen, pausing there, waiting for François, the chef, to notice her and invite them in. General manager or not, she didn't invade the chef's territory without permission.

Immensely relieved at having something else to discuss, she said, "I don't remember everyone, and I'll let you in on a trade secret. When a reservation is made, Mai runs the name through the computer to see if the guest is a repeater. If so, she writes me up a card with personal details like physical description, the number of the room they occupied last, likes and dislikes of the guests, and any other comments we might have felt were appropriate. That way I can greet people by name, mention little things that happened during their previous visit, and sometimes even tell them who else is here again whom they might remember. It makes people feel like members of an exclusive club."

He laughed softly. "So you cheat."

She was indignant. "I do not cheat! It's important for people to feel like insiders, and my remembering them is the best way I know to ensure that they do. Often I do remember them, like the Colliers. The cards are just reminders if required."

"What do you mean, feel like insiders?"

"Um . . . if you see a sign saying No Entry: Authorized Personnel Only, doesn't it bother you?"

He laughed again. "No. Not particularly. Why should it? What do I care what goes on in back rooms? It's probably stuff I wouldn't care about if I did get to see it."

"Not everyone feels that way. I don't. I hate signs like that. They shut people out, they point out that there are some who can and others who can't. I want my establishment to be a place where no one ever feels excluded. All my guests are 'authorized personnel,' and if my remembering people who have been here before makes them feel as if they are among the chosen few, members of the in crowd, part of the family, then that is my aim in business. If I let anyone feel shut out, then I'm failing them. Failing myself."

He looked down at her earnest face and suddenly he wanted to hold her close, to draw her into the circle of his arms, to make sure she never felt left out or shut out or not part of the family ever again. What had that guy, Kevin, said? They had been brother and sister for a bit? Foster children? Sure, that answered a lot of questions for him, questions Jacquie always managed to evade with a laugh or a change of subject or even a cold, forbidding stare. Questions she had evaded again this evening. He wanted to hold her, but he wanted to shake her too. Did she think it would matter to him if she was a child from a broken home?

He contented himself with taking her hand in his and wrapping his fingers tightly around it as the chef, looking harried, came bustling toward them, wiping his hands on a large white towel.

"Madame Knight. Réne. I am honored. Please, come in. Will you sample this sauce for me, madame? It is, I believe, superb, but I would like your opinion."

Jacquie solemnly tasted and pronounced the sauce exactly as François had described it. She duly admired the massive baron of beef, inhaled appreciatively the aroma of fried chicken, peeked into bubbling pots and nodded approvingly before she made her way back to the swinging doors, the ritual completed. François would have been in-

sulted if she had not put in an appearance and been effusively complimentary. At her side, she noticed Renny was munching on a crusty slice from the end of a fresh loaf of bread.

Shaking her head, she smiled, wondering which one of the female kitchen staff he had charmed it from. There was no doubt about it. This man she was married to had more charm than he knew what to do with. Maybe that was why he made a career out of spreading it around so liberally. Was that what he'd been doing earlier, out there under the tree? Just being charming? Or had the expression in his eyes meant more? Did he really want to know about her? And knowing, would he change? She sighed.

He pulled out her chair for her, and as she sat, his fingertips rested lightly on her shoulders for a moment, then moved to brush the back of her neck briefly.

"Tired?" he asked.

She nodded. "A little." It was as good an excuse as any to explain her sigh. The truth was, she was confused and unhappy and wished she knew where her life was going. She wasn't used to having such ambivalent feelings. She wasn't used to anyone wanting her to discuss her past. She just plain wasn't used to sharing her house and her life with anyone, let alone a man whose most casual touch set her senses atingle, and whose most casual question terrified her to the verge of panic.

She knew she was kidding herself if she tried to

pretend that his questioning had been casual. He really did want her to talk about her past. After the things he'd heard Kevin say, she was certain Renny was just biding his time before he demanded to have the blanks filled in. Was she going to do it? She didn't know. She twisted her hands in her lap as he sat down across from her and lifted the menu. She didn't even look at hers. How could she possibly choose what she wanted to eat when she still had to choose whether or not to tell Renny her secrets and suffer the consequences?

Later she realized she must have ordered something, because a plate was set in front of her, and she ate some of the rare roast beef. She was sipping coffee when Renny said, "Let's go home, Jac. We don't have to stay and dance, do we?"

Her heart lurched. She knew why he wanted to go home—to grill her. His silence so far had only been a result of his good breeding. *We do not have personal discussions in public. If we have a skeleton in our closet, we must keep it to ourselves.* She was sure Renny had been taught those golden rules by his parents. Brother, did she have a skeleton!

But what could she say? She'd already told him she was tired. How could she back out of that now and say she wanted to stay and dance? She couldn't.

"Of course we don't have to stay and dance," she said. "But you'll be breaking a lot of hearts if you don't. There's no need for you to go home just because I'm tired. We don't have to carry our charade that far."

He lifted his hand and ran a very deliberate, very evocative caress from her left temple to her chin, and then rubbed the pad of a thumb over her mouth. "I think I'm tired of playing charades," he said. "And something tells me you are too."

She said nothing, she wasn't capable of speaking. Her voice was trapped beneath the sudden wild pounding of her heart in her throat.

Suddenly she was more fearful than she had ever been in her life.

It took her a few minutes to get a grip on herself. All right, he had called it. The time was now, and he was right. She was as tired as he was of playing charades with him. She loved him, and now, tonight, she was going to show him. Tonight, she was going to invite him into her bed just as graciously as she knew how. She met his gaze and realized—he knew.

A shiver of fear blended with anticipation prickled her arms, raising goose bumps. He saw them, smiled, and smoothed them from her skin. She wondered what he would do if she acted like a wimp again. Would he continue, maybe force her to overcome whatever had cooled her ardor the last time, or would he stop? Oh, Lord, what if he stopped again? She couldn't let herself think of failure, think of having to stop.

First, they had to start.

Even before they began, however, she had to make sure he knew exactly who Jacqueline Train was—and who she was not. Fear rose in great, choking spasms inside her. She knew she had to fight off her fears and force herself to go through with telling Renny. Because once before she had made the mistake of putting off telling the man she loved, and when she was finally forced to, when his parents had had her investigated and confronted her with the truth, he had left her.

She wondered why it was so important for her to tell him now, when it hadn't seemed necessary before they got married. They weren't committing themselves to anything but a temporary alliance then, she reasoned.

Did that mean deep down she thought they were doing something different this time? Did that mean that somewhere inside her she was beginning to hope there was a small chance he wouldn't take off in the end?

She looked at him, and didn't know.

He took her hand and stood, his gaze on her face, his mouth taut with the same kind of tension she felt quivering along her muscles, and they made their way slowly through the dining room, saying good night, explaining that they had a prior commitment, otherwise they'd have loved to stay and party with their guests.

The snow had stopped falling by the time they emerged from the lodge to walk home. It lay underfoot in a thick soft blanket of powder that formed sparkling clouds as they waded through it.

"The powder on the upper slopes will be fantastic in the morning," said Jacqueline, more to break the brittle silence between them than because she cared about the snow conditions.

"Right," said Renny, as if relieved to have something to discuss. "And if I have any pull around here, I intend to be on the first chair up."

"I have an in with the hill manager," she said, "so if anybody gets the first chair, it'll most likely be me."

He took her gloved hand and stripped it bare before shoving it into his pocket wrapped in his own. It was such a strangely intimate thing to do that it took her breath away.

"Wanna bet?" he challenged. "For your information, lady, I have an in with the hotel manager. Maybe my pull is even stronger than yours."

"Could be," she granted. "But rather than put it to the test, why don't we agree to share the first chair up?"

He came to a halt and stared down at her. "Why, Mrs. Knight, could you be asking me for a date?"

Again a prickle swept over her arms, tightened her nipples, and heated her insides.

"If I were, would you be interested?" She was very still as she waited for his reply.

"More than interested." His voice was a soft, low rumble. It thrilled her.

"Oh." She continued to look up at him.

"I'm interested in more than a date, and if you don't quit looking at me like that, I can't guarantee I can maintain a friendly distance until we get safely inside," he warned her.

The fluttering inside her grew stronger, became a tremor that threatened to knock her knees out from under her. "Is that a fact?" she said.

"Yup. A fact."

Her look dared him to go further, she knew it did. But she wanted so much to kiss him just once before risking losing him completely that she continued to look at him—and was rewarded.

His kiss was as potent as she had remembered it could be, and it sent a rush of delight flooding through her. His lips were cold on the outside, warm on the inside, and flavored slightly with brandy and mint. Impulsively she licked his top lip, wanting more of the taste of him, and he growled a warning sound. For a moment she considered not heeding it, but then, with a regretful sigh, she retreated. They had a long way to go yet tonight. A very long way to go.

But first she had to ask him an extremely important question. "Renny, would you do me the honor of sharing my bed tonight?" she asked, and her voice only shook a tad.

She saw him swallow, saw him close his eyes briefly as if possibly sending up a prayer of thanks. A smile formed on his face, crinkled his eyes, curved his mouth, and grooved his cheeks as it grew wider and wider.

"That," he said softly, "was the most gracious and welcome invitation I have ever had. I accept, Jacqueline." This time his kiss was deep and promising, and still much too short.

Back in the chalet he stoked the fire they had

left banked in the stove, went to the small bar and poured himself another brandy, and then looked at her for the first time since they'd kissed outside, lifting the bottle toward her in invitation. If he was in any hurry to start making love to her, he wasn't showing it, and she was grateful.

She acknowledged his salute and nodded, and then said, "Renny? Don't think I've changed my mind. I haven't. But . . . first, I think we need to talk. Okay?"

He hesitated for only a fraction of a second. "What do we need to talk about, Jacquie?"

"Me."

He stood very quietly watching her through narrowed eyes. "Sure. Mind if I change out of my suit and tie?"

Jacquie went up the stairs to change from her dress into something more comfortable as well, and came back to find him wearing a track suit similar to the one she had slipped into.

He was sitting on the couch and reached out a hand to her, pulling her down beside him. Lifting her snifter, he handed her the aromatic drink and sat quietly sipping and inhaling his own, vitally aware of the warmth of her body near his, of the constant tremor running through her. Setting down his glass, he put both arms around her and said, "Go ahead, Jac. What do you want to tell me?"

"I . . ." She didn't want to tell him anything, but she had to. She had to tell him the whole truth. "I don't quite know where to start," she said lamely. As she sipped, her glass clattered against her teeth.

He took the drink from her and set it beside his own, tilted her face up, and scanned it with compassionate eyes. "Hey, we're friends, Jac. Don't be scared. Can't you trust me enough to believe that no matter what you have to tell me, it won't change how much I like you? Why don't you start by answering a question for me?"

"What question?"

Lord! he thought. She looked as if she were going to her doom! He let her chin go, and she lowered her face. "Just this one, honey," he said. "Who was Mr. Train?"

Her head jerked up. "What?"

"Your friend Kevin called you Jacquie Jensen. Yet when I met you, you were Jacquie Train. Stands to reason there must have been a Mr. Train."

She looked back down and shook her head.

"There was no Mr. Train," she said, and then stopped. She drew in a deep breath and let it out slowly. "I . . . wanted a name that was all my own, that really belonged to me, not one that had been assigned to me by a social worker who pulled it out of a hat or off a list or out of thin air. Elliot. That was what they called me. Jacqueline Elliot. It must have been the week for *E*'s. If I'd arrived one week earlier, I could have been Jacqueline Davis. One week later, maybe Jacqueline French. Or what if it had been even later in the year, and they'd gone all the way down to the *X*'s? What would they have done then? I . . . Oh, that doesn't matter. I wanted to be a real person with a real identity, and I was on a train when I made the decision to name myself. Jacqueline Train sounded a hell of a lot easier to handle than Jacqueline Clickety-Clack, though I've always thought hyphenated names have a certain . . . cachet."

Her voice broke and the look she slanted at him was defiant and challenging. He returned it calmly and stayed silent. Someone had *assigned* her a name? Surely even if she was "illegitimate" she would have had her mother's name?

When she didn't speak, he prodded her gently. "So you were on a train when you chose your name. Then what?"

"I . . . Renny, I'm sorry, but I can't go on. I'm going to bed, are you joining me?" she said in a rush as she leaped to her feet and flung herself away from him, heading for the stairs at a dead run.

"Jacqueline!" His voice crackled after her.

She halted halfway up and stood waiting, not turning, her body rigid. To the back of her head he said quietly, "You're a coward. You're running away. If you think I'll follow you and act as if none of this matters, you're wrong. I'm not going to follow you."

"All right." Her voice was like a whisper and he suspected she was close to tears. He steeled himself against relenting. Dammit, she had to talk to him!

"Don't you want to know why?"

She nodded, and turned to look at him. Her face was a white mask out of which enormous aqua eyes gazed at him, beseeching him. "You want me to know, so tell me."

He kept his feet planted on the floor so he wouldn't fly up the stairs and clasp her to him, so he wouldn't give in to her need—and his.

"Because we can't go any further until you tell me about Jacqueline Train," he said in a taut voice. "I can't go on, Jac."

"If I did tell you, we wouldn't go any further anyway," she said quietly. "So what's the point? Good night, Ren." She didn't wait for an answer.

He didn't give her one. For a long time he sat, sipping brandy, thinking, wondering if she were up there crying, wanting to go to her, but knowing that for both their sakes, she was the one who had to come to him.

Seven

He'd been in bed for nearly an hour when he heard her get up. If she was trying to be quiet, she wasn't succeeding.

He heard her come down the stairs, put on her boots, and go out the door. She was going to her pool, of course. Was she hoping he would follow her? He lay rigid, knowing that he had to be strong enough to withstand his almost irresistible compulsion to go after her. He would withstand it. He would.

She had done as he asked, hadn't she? he realized. She had found the courage to ask him to go to bed with her. Had that taken all the courage she possessed? Was he asking too much of her all at once? Did he absolutely have to know about her past? It couldn't make any difference, could it? He groaned and sat up, burying his face in his hands. Damn, but she had him in worse shape than he had ever been in his life! Swinging his feet over the side of his bed, he reached for his pants.

She was stripping off her clothes when he arrived at the edge of the glade. Quickly, unselfconsciously, with economical yet graceful movements, she pulled her sweatshirt off over her head, skinned her track pants down over her legs and stepped out of them. Standing first on one foot and then on the other, she peeled off her socks. She unhooked her bra and let it slide down her arms and fall on top of the heap of clothing at her feet. Then, as he held his breath, she slipped her panties off the curve of her buttocks and slid them down her legs.

He was trembling, watching her body unwrapped until she stood like a slim marble statue wreathed in mist.

More lovely than he had remembered, with the moon silvering her skin, catching unexpected glints from her shining hair, she stood there for a moment. As her gleaming body played peek-a-boo within the shielding shreds of fog floating around her like the veils of an exotic dancer, she reached her arms up and stretched, her breasts lifting high. His head swam as he watched her, longing to go to her but rendered immobile by a kind of uncertainty that was alien to him. Had her lack of stealth indeed been a subtle invitation? Would she be standing there naked under the moon, clad only in mist, the blackness of her hair outlined against the whiteness of the snow, if she hadn't expected him to follow? Did she know, even now, that he was watching? No! She didn't know. Her very lack of self-consciousness told him so. He wasn't ready for her to know, not yet.

Oh, Lord, was she even real? Maybe he was asleep and dreaming. Had she bewitched him? Was she the elf he had called her, immune to human feelings such as sensations of cold so she could strip naked in the middle of a snowy glade? Could she as easily fly into the heat of the sun? Was she more than the mist through which she shimmered?

Was she really the woman he thought he remembered? Her passion, her heat, her wild desire only he could slake, did they still exist? Or had he killed all that by his clumsiness, his inability to deal with her insecurities, and his own?

The need to go to her was almost more than he could bear, but he continued to stand and watch her, unseen, as he had watched the other night until an owl had attracted her attention. He saw her step down—off a platform of some kind—until the water rose around her waist. Half turning toward him, she stepped down yet again, and he felt his heartbeat quicken as he saw the pale, lovely shapes of her breasts floating voluptuously on the dark water.

When she lay back and stroked with her arms across the pool to a shallower spot and reclined there, her arms and legs floating free on the surface, her shape a mystery as the fog closed in on her, he had to fight to swallow. In that moment, he knew that he loved her. It came over him in such a rush that he nearly passed out.

He stood staring at her ethereal shape for a long moment, trying to make sense of his new discovery. He loved her! The idea was outrageous. Renny Knight did not fall in love. Women fell in love with him, or claimed to, but he never reciprocated the feeling. He liked women, sure. Some he liked more than others. Some he had wanted, but he'd never wanted anyone with the same intensity as he wanted Jacqueline Train. Because he loved her? Of course! he realized.

Suddenly, it was so clear and so simple he wanted to laugh and shout his discovery aloud. He was in love with his wife, with the woman who used his name, who had once been pregnant with his child, and he thought he might burst with the need for her to be pregnant again.

He *had* to give her more babies, to give her the kind of happiness he knew she was capable of fceling. It was the reason why he had been born, and it had taken him all this time to understand it!

What was it she'd said? A love so big it had no place to go but into the creation of a new human being? What he felt for her was a love that big. He wanted to go to her, gather her close, soothe her every fear, tell her there was no need for worries, or loneliness, or demons. He would love her and protect her and cherish her forever, and make her life complete, but . . . Could he make such a promise? He loved her now, he might even love her a year from now—or in fifty years. He had never loved anyone before, he didn't *know*.

Did love last? Could it last as long as she would need it to? Could he destroy her if he promised her something and then had to break his promise? He had never known anyone with needs as vast as hers, needs he suspected he might never fully understand. The responsibility of it filled him with awe. Did she love him too? She wanted him. But love?

He stood studying her face in the silver light. He wanted to tell her how he felt. He wanted to ask her if she loved him. Yet the answer she might give terrified him.

He was scared to death. If he had the sense God gave a duck, he'd turn and walk away. Oh, hell! Who was he trying to kid? He'd never walk away from the women he loved when she was lying naked in a warm, secret hot spring in the middle of the night. No man could walk away under those circumstances. What he should do was ski boldly out of the shadows. He should kick free of his bindings, stab his skis into the snow beside hers, and strip naked too. He should wade into that pool with her and make love to her until she couldn't think, and then *tell* her that she loved him as much as he loved her.

So what in the hell was he doing standing cold

and alone in the shadows while Jacqueline was warm and just as alone in the pool?

"You're welcome to come and join me, Ren," she said, with what he thought was a note of uncertainty in her voice. "Or isn't that why you came?"

His breath left his lungs in a whoosh. "There's a flat rock where I left my things," she continued quietly. "It's warm there."

"Oh, hell," he said softly, not moving from his shadowy spot between the trees. How long had she known of his presence? And of course she had seen him last night. He thought with sudden embarrassment of his faked snoring when she got home. He felt like the foolish, abashed eleven-year-old he'd been when he'd got caught peeking in his big sister's bedroom window.

He was a lot more than eleven now, though, and his embarrassment was something he was going to have to live with. Because, for the first time in his life, there was a woman he didn't think he could live without. With three swift pushes and glides he was at the side of the pool. He kicked free of his skis and stepped through the curtain of mist onto the flat rock. He was only two yards away from her now, and wisps of steam still kept floating between them, hiding her expression.

He cleared his throat. "If I come into your pool, water sprite, I'm going to make love to you. Is that still what you want?" He felt awkward, inept, vulnerable. He heard his voice shake and despised himself for revealing such weakness.

The pounding of his own pulse in his ears muffled any inflection that might have been in her tone, but he heard her say, "It's what I want." Then, as a puff of a breeze cleared the air between them, he saw her sitting cross-legged in a foot of water, watching him. "I made sure you heard me tonight, Ren, in the hope that you'd follow me again, in spite of what you said back in the house."

Her voice cracked slightly on the last word, and his heart ached with love. She wasn't as cool and detached as she was trying to pretend. She was as nervous and as vulnerable as he. A great wave of tenderness swept over him. Oh, Lord, was he up to this? Was he strong enough to love a woman like Jacqueline Train? A woman who tried so hard to show the world she didn't care what was handed out to her, but who wept inside and had been forced to find a name for herself because she didn't feel she really owned the one she had?

He stood staring at her ethereal shape for a long moment, wondering if he would ever fully plumb the depths of his feelings for her, ever learn to handle the magnitude of the emotions she could send sweeping through him.

His fingers felt clumsy and much too large as he fumbled with his zipper, dropped his jacket beside hers, and then sat down to pull off his boots. Standing again, he slowly undid the buttons on his shirt, shrugged out of it, pulled his T-shirt from the waist of his pants, and then stopped. She waded to the rock and stood waiting for him.

"Renny? What made you . . . change your mind?"

Her voice was low, hardly above a whisper, and in it he detected a note of fear. What was she asking him? If his appearance tonight meant that he intended to force answers from her?

He wanted to hold her to him, kiss away whatever doubts she might have about herself, about him, and promise never to demand anything she didn't feel able to give.

And he would. If he could ever get his damned clothes off.

It had never been difficult for him to undress in front of a woman. He took pride in his body. He knew it was long and strong and lean and good to look at, but was it everything *Jacqueline* had ever dreamed of? That question took on enormous importance in his mind. Was she comparing him to someone else? If so, did he please her? He watched her face for signs of approval—or disapproval. He'd been naked before in front of her, so why did he have this terrible need for reassurance? He wasn't a green kid, he only felt like one.

Oh, Lord, did she love him? he wondered. Even a little? She had to!

He pulled off his T-shirt and dropped it, feeling her gaze on his chest. When he slipped out of his jeans and dumped them onto the heap of discarded clothing, she took one step closer and touched his ankle as if she couldn't help herself. Her fingers closed over his skin—and wrapped around his heart. He shivered.

"Are you cold?" she whispered.

"No," he said, studying her face in the silver

light. "No." She hadn't turned away. She didn't look as if the sight of him disgusted her, but she didn't look particularly pleased either. She was simply—waiting.

He wanted to tell her how much he loved her, but his throat closed up and he couldn't speak. She was so lovely, yet so remote. If she was only willing to share her body with him, he didn't think he'd be able to stand it. He knew now how much more he had to ask of her.

"You're shivering," she said.

"I'm shaking. I want you, Jacqueline."

"I know," she said, and stepped back, giving him room, taking the warmth of her hand from his ankle. He felt the loss throughout his entire body.

With one swift motion, he slid his bikini briefs down over his legs and dropped them, still watching her face. She smiled, and he could breathe again.

She reached up a hand to him and took his in a warm clasp. "Step down and then turn a bit before coming any farther," she said, guiding him. "The water's over my head on the left of the rock. It might not be over yours, but I'd rather you not find out in the dark. It's warm, isn't it?"

She spoke as she might have to a child, or to a casual friend, not as if she were speaking to a naked man who had just told her that he was going to make love to her. Was it because it didn't matter to her if he did or did not? Or was she always casual with her lovers?

Immersed up to his ribs, he let go of her hand and stood, feeling the water swirl around him as his doubts swirled, feeling it bubbling against his skin the way bubbles of excitement and desire tingled in his blood. "Jac, I didn't come . . . prepared." He hadn't been thinking, he'd only been reacting—to the memory of her misty shape as he'd seen it last night, as he'd remembered it all day, as he'd visualized it when he heard her go out again and had followed.

"I did," she said. It was as if the admission unlocked something in her. Words came tumbling out, her voice high, breathless. "Not that I was sure you'd come. I know you've wanted to—to come to me, since you got here, but you were waiting for me to ask you. I wanted to ask you, Ren. You must know that. But I've been so afraid of an . . . involvement with you. I . . . try not to get involved." Her smile was crooked. "Because I don't have even an elf or a leprechaun in my background. I don't have a background."

"Jacquie—"

She would not be interrupted. She covered his lips with her fingertips, soft, warm pads that he ached to kiss. They trembled against his flesh.

"I want you to know that I'll never try to hold you to anything permanent," she said. "I promise you I'm not looking for permanency any more than you are."

He snatched her hand down. "Jacquie, you're—" You're wrong, he was going to say, but she wouldn't let him continue.

"Please!" she broke in. "Let me finish." She went on, each word stabbing another knife into him until he reeled with pain of it.

"I won't try to trap you, because that would mean trapping myself. I do want you, Ren. So much! I want what we had before. But like you, I know I won't want it forever. Just until—one of us doesn't want it anymore. When that happens for you, you have to promise to tell me, as I'll tell you if it happens for me first. Okay?"

Somehow, he managed to take a page out of her book and hide his feelings behind a bland mask if not of indifference, then at least of studied control. Lord, here was a woman giving him exactly what he'd always wished for—freedom to pack up and leave whenever he chose, offering him a way out when he was finished with the relationship. Before it had been right for him, only this time it was wrong. And he believed it was wrong for her too.

He loved this woman! He wanted her! Yet even standing naked with her in a secluded hot spring in the middle of the night, knowing she wanted him, he couldn't tell her how he felt. Her devastating words had robbed him of the strength to so much as raise his hand to touch her. If he touched her now, she would see how hard he trembled. Until "one of us" doesn't want it anymore? And which one would that be? Not him, by God!

Had she had this same conversation with other men? Her voice was so cool, so controlled, so detached. She was bargaining: You promise me this, and I'll promise you that. Were they about to embark on a love affair, or were they forming a union contract? he wondered.

"All those nights—when you left the chalet. Where were you going?" Pain rasped in his voice, but . . oh, hell, he had to know!

"Why, here," she said. "Where else?"

"I didn't know. I—wondered."

"I haven't been sleeping," she said.

"I haven't either." He hesitated, then rushed on. "I thought when you went out that you were going to another man. I stayed awake each time until you came back. And I still wanted you."

"Until last night?"

"You mean, when I found you here? I wanted you then, believe me. You were the most beautiful thing I had ever seen. It was so hard to leave." His voice shook with the force of his emotion.

"Then why did you leave?" Hurt caused her voice to tremble. She cleared her throat and said quickly, "No. Forget that. You don't have to answer to me. You're free to do as you wish." Again, he was caught in an upsurge of love for her. She was so soft, so tender, and so determined not to show it.

"I felt as if I were . . . intruding on something private," he said. "If this pool were something you wanted other people to know about, you would make it available to your guests. If you wanted me to stay, why didn't you speak to me then the way you did tonight?"

He sucked in a sharp breath when her fingertips grazed the hair on his chest. His body leaped to attention. He squeezed his eyes shut.

"I wasn't sure it was you. I didn't know who else it could have been, but I wasn't positive until I found your tracks in the woods, and they led home. Then I knew. I . . . wished that you'd stayed."

He opened his eyes and caught sight of her trembling lower lip and bent to capture it for an instant between his. Lifting his head, he flattened her hand on his chest, holding it over his hammering heart. "And when you got home? You must have known I wasn't sleeping. You could have—come in."

Why hadn't she gone to him?—because she hadn't been invited. She shrugged, and her breasts bobbed in the water.

He lifted his free hand and stroked it up under one breast, unable to resist. This time, it was her breath that caught, and her nipple peaked suddenly, followed by its mate a second later.

"You were pretending to snore." Her voice was unsteady, but her gaze never faltered. "You didn't want me to know you had followed. Maybe because you didn't want me."

"I've always wanted you," he assured her huskily, bending and touching one of her temptingly hard nipples with his tongue. "Salty," he murmured against her flesh. "But so sweet."

"Yes." Her voice was little more than a sigh as she wrapped her hands around his head and leaned back to lift her breasts higher for him.

Then as he drew the nipple into his mouth and slowly increased the strength of his suckling, her voice rose in a question. "Ren? What if . . . ?"

He knew what she was asking. He lifted his head, his hands on her shoulders, his gaze sweeping over her upper body, then meeting her beseeching eyes. "It's all right, love," he said. "We'll be just fine."

"Yes." She thought they would, thought she would. "Touch me again, Renny. Kiss my breasts."

"I will," he promised, sliding his hands around her narrow waist. "Come closer, Jac. Touch me with your body. I need to be touched as much as you do. Put your arms around me."

He cradled her against him, her breasts flattened on his chest, feeling the hardness of her nipples pressing into his flesh. He slid his palms down over her wet, slick back, cupped her buttocks, and moved her against his own hardness. "We're going to take it as slow as you want, Jacquie. We won't do anything you're not ready to do. And if all you want is for us to hold each other, then that'll be enough for me. If your—wanting—dies again, we'll simply wait until next time, or the time after, when maybe it won't. Don't worry. Relax and let happen whatever is going to happen for us."

To reassure her, he lightened his embrace, stroking her back with long, steady movements. He hoped he could stick to his promise, and when she let her hands rise from his back to his nape, her thumbs caressing the skin below his ears, he doubted he could.

She pressed her hands against the back of his head and tugged him down toward her. He lowered his face to her uptilted one, kissing her softly over and over again on her eyelids, her forehead, her cheeks, and the corners of her mouth.

When she groaned, "Ren, please!" he finally took her mouth, finding it open and soft and yearning.

For endless moments he contented himself with kisses that drugged them both. His tongue was hard then soft against hers, twisting with it, stroking the roof of her mouth, lapping at the sweet pool underneath, growing hotter and hotter until her tongue was as insistent as his, her hands as demanding on his body, her breath as ragged and broken as his own.

His hands kneaded her breasts possessively, and she reveled in his touch, rising to it, her head falling back as she moaned and spoke his name in a faraway voice she scarcely recognized as hers. "Oh, how I love the feel of your mouth on me," she said.

With a growl of delight, he drew one nipple deep inside his mouth, while his finger and thumb tugged at the other one. His hand slid down her body, over the slight roundness of her stomach, and into the soft wetness between her thighs. Even the water could not dilute the thick, satiny moisture of her desire, and he stroked his fingers over her again and again until she was gasping, writhing, and her legs floated up around his waist of their own volition, capturing him in a heavenly prison.

"Jac . . . be sure, love," he said into her neck, but he knew that if she tried to pull back now, it would be far, far too late for him to stop.

He had no need to worry. Her voice was thick with longing when she said, "I'm sure . . . I'm sure. I need you. Come into me, Renny . . . Oh, Lord, yes!"

She cried out as he entered her in a heated rush, his hands cupping her bottom, her thighs wrapped tightly around him as they rode the waves that rose around them, within them. He rocked her against him, kissing her deeply, and she clung to him with her arms and legs and lips. She wasn't aware any longer of any separate sensations, it was all a rushing, roaring tidal wave that carried them over the peak and down the other side.

Eight

Renny slowly became aware that she was still wrapped around him, that his head was pressed to her breasts as she stroked his hair murmuring soft, tender words to him. The rock they'd left their clothing on was cutting into his back, and his legs were so weak that if it hadn't been for the buoyancy provided by the mineral water, he would have sunk. Reluctantly, she let her legs float down until her feet were on top of his.

He lifted his head, cupped her face in his hands, and kissed her, caught up in a wondrous afterglow that he knew would live on in his heart forever. Overcome by tenderness such as he had never known, he buried his face against her hair, breathing in her scent and the briny mineral tang of the pool. Always, for eternity, he knew, salty air would conjure up memories of this time with Jacqueline, this time of perfect harmony, of love.

"I've dreamed of holding you again, Jac. Of loving you." Why had it taken him so long to realize the element missing in his life? It was love, and love was synonymous with Jacqueline.

"Me too." Her hand shook on his face and he realized her whole body was atremble, that she was having difficulty standing too. Lifting her, he carried her to the shallow rock where he had seen her reclining earlier. Kneeling, he laid her back into the warm water and stretched out beside her, loving the way she continued to touch him gently, kiss his temple, his eyebrows, move her soft, wet hands over his body as if trying to memorize his form. She paused now and then to scoop up handfuls of warm water and spill it down over his back. "All I had dreamed of, too, Ren. And I did dream of making love to you. So many times." She smiled wryly and added, "Even before you came back. And after—Lord, every night I went crazy thinking of you being so close, hearing you downstairs. Renny, don't sleep down there again, okay? Sleep with me. Make love to me every night. Take me home now and make love to me there. My bed is so big and so empty without you," she added breathlessly, her lips moving over his chest and stomach, back up to his throat, seeking his mouth and the potent kisses they shared together.

"Loving you," he had said, and had meant the words literally. But she had said "making love to you." It hadn't meant the same for her. She considered it just a pleasuring of the senses, not a swelling of the heart. He drew her to him, holding her fiercely, kissing her over and over as if trying to tell her without words that what he was doing was a world apart from merely "making love."

"Oh, sweetheart," he whispered when he finally had to come up for air. "My water sprite. My pointy-eared elf."

He kissed her ears, lingering on their unique outline until she gasped his name, twisting herself around until her mouth found his and clung, demandingly, as she arched into the curve of his body.

"Tell me," he said against her breasts, feeling his own control sliding from him as hers was escaping her hold. "What are you? Some kind of enchantress?"

"A woman," she gasped. "A woman who . . . Renny, please, don't talk now. I want you so much!"

"A woman who what?" he demanded. "A woman who loves me?"

She didn't reply, and her stroking, squeezing touch was more than he could bear. He could hold back no longer. Lifting her over him, he plunged inside her, moving her until their rhythm became synchronized, and the deep spasms began within her body, inciting his own release.

Later, they dried each other with the one towel she had brought, dressed, and skied home side by side.

"Will you . . . be with me?" she asked hesitantly at the foot of the stairs, her gaze on his face.

He touched her cheek with one hand. "Always," he said.

Always? Silently she echoed his word, and silently she rejected it. She knew it wasn't true.

She said nothing, though, and took his hand, leading him up to her loft and her warm feather bed.

Sitting with her back against the headboard, her face pale and sober, she said, "Ren, I think I should finish telling you the story of Jacqueline Elliot Train."

He brushed her hair back from her face and stroked her ear. "No. I don't need to know anymore. It hurts you to talk about it, Jac. I can see that. And above all, I don't want you to be hurt."

What right did he have to expect perfect candor from her when he had secrets of his own? he asked himself. It weighed so heavily on him, that secret, and he thought about telling her, considered what her reaction would be, and flinched inwardly. No. If he told her, he'd never stand a chance of convincing her he loved her and wanted to have children with her more than he had ever wanted anything else. Oh, Lord, as hard as it would be, he had to keep it to himself. There was no way she would ever find out, be hurt by it. Silence was best.

"Jac, I . . ."

I love you. He wanted so much to say it, but feeling it and saying it were two different things. If he had any hope that she felt the same, maybe it would be easier, but he had no such hope—only a deep and abiding need to do what was right for Jacqueline. He didn't think something as painful as talking about her childhood seemed to be for her could be right.

She pulled a corner of the comforter up over her back and hitched herself around until she sat, cross-legged, facing him. "I . . . want you to know," she said.

He knew he could stop her if he chose. He knew if he were to reach out and pull her into his arms, she would come to him unresisting, and in moments they both would have forgotten that she had a tale to tell.

He nodded slowly, while his heart beat out a painful rhythm in his chest. What did she have to say that could be so bad it would make her look the way she looked now? he wondered. Maybe she was right, maybe she had to tell him so they could put it behind them and grow closer from this point onward.

"Tell me, then," he said quietly.

She swallowed once, licked her lips, and began. "My first home was a cardboard box." Her tone was flat, but her gaze held the challenging, defiant look he'd seen earlier, as if she expected to show shock or perhaps disgust. He simply continued to watch her face, keeping his own bland and expressionless. After a moment, she went on.

"A man was seen placing the box on the backseat of a double-parked taxi. The driver had gone into a coffee shop for a Danish. He came out to find a naked newborn baby waiting for him. He took me to a hospital and ran, probably because he was afraid they might hold him responsible for the cost of my care." She paused, searched Ren's face, and frowned at what she saw there—or didn't see.

"I can see his point," said Renny. "It was a valid concern."

"Uh . . . yes. I guess it was." Jacquie stared at him. Okay, so maybe he wasn't going to pull the shocked and outraged act, or the even more insulting disbelieving one, or the patronizing "hey, kid, I don't care that you're a bastard" bit.

"A nun christened me Jacqueline after her favorite sister." She smiled a terrible, bitter smile that made him ache inside. "I've always been glad her sister's name wasn't Gertrude."

"Hmm." He smiled back at her, gave into temptation, and reached out to take her hand. He stroked her fingers, then linked them with his own. "Or Blanch."

"Yeah. Or how about Maude? Or Myrtle?" They both laughed quietly, and he saw her defiance fade.

"What if her sister had had a cute name like Fifi, or Boopsie or Bubbles? It could have changed your whole life," he suggested. "You might have ended up on the stage."

Jacquie knew it was up to her to decide if she wanted to go on talking. He was making it easy for her to stop whenever she wanted—and he wasn't, so far, recoiling from her.

She went on.

"It took the authorities a year or so to decide

that they weren't going to find the man who had dumped me in the cab, or the woman who had given birth to me. By then, they realized my crooked foot, which they'd hoped might straighten out on its own, was going to have to be corrected with surgery and therapy. When that was all over, and I was pronounced whole and fit and suitable for adoption, I was four and a half years old, had lived in seven foster homes, and was, by all accounts, a little monster. Adoptive parents didn't exactly break down the doors trying to get me.

"When I was eight I was made part of an experiment in moving inner-city kids out into the country into a more 'wholesome' atmosphere in an attempt to stem the rising tide of delinquency in welfare children. I was sent to a place in upstate New York called Elephant Mountain. By the standards of the mountains around here it was a little bump of a hill, but at least I learned to ski there. The people who ran it were the Jensens."

"Oh. They adopted you?"

"Uh-uh. But we all—there were four of us, Kevin, Sarah, June, and me—used the Jensens's name. They preferred it for some reason."

"Maybe they thought it would give you more of a sense of belonging," he suggested, but she only smiled noncommittally.

"I did not want to be there," she said. "I was angry and resentful and terrified. Do you know that until I went to Elephant Mountain, I didn't know it ever got completely dark at night? It was the most frightening experience I'd ever had, to wake up and not be able to see absolutely anything. Of course, I screamed bloody murder."

"And got a night-light, I hope."

"No night-light. Because I was so scared, I lit a match so I could find a light switch. The Jensens then discovered and took away my last pack of cigarettes, and I had no idea where I was going to be able to steal more in the wilderness I'd been sentenced to."

Ren gaped at her, reacting for the first time. It pleased her strangely to have gotten a rise out of him.

"Cigarettes? You were eight years old and stealing smokes? No wonder they wanted to get you out of town and into a more wholesome atmosphere."

"Wholesome was not what I wanted. I ran away."

"You get far?"

She shook her head and grinned at the memory. "Not far at all. I sneaked out of the room I shared with June and Sarah, slid down the roof and onto a snowdrift. Halfway down the drive, which was pretty long and incredibly dark, I found half a cigarette and some matches in the pocket of my jacket. I stopped to light up. Someone saw the flare of my match and came out to investigate. It was about three in the morning.

"That someone was Eric Sorensen. He grabbed the butt out of my mouth, flung it onto the ground and stomped on it. I went at him, kicking and clawing and screaming. I could cuss better than any longshoreman. Eric told me to stop. I didn't, so he picked me up, turned me over his knee, and swatted my bottom with three good, hard whacks. I bit his thumb—drew blood too," she added proudly.

Ren winced. "And earned yourself another whack or two?"

"No." Her hand was still linked with his and she tightened her fingers unconsciously, staring at an imaginary point somewhere beyond Ren, staring back into a past he knew he would never fully comprehend. "No, Eric gave me something I'd never gotten from anyone else. He sat down on the snowback that had been plowed out of the driveway and held me on his lap while I howled and carried on. He rocked me and crooned nice things to me until I settled down. Then he kissed me and told me everything was going to be fine. His was the first lap I ever remember sitting on. From that moment on, I was Eric Sorensen's creature."

After several minutes during which the only sounds were the crackling of the fire downstairs and the angry rasping of Ren's breath, he glared ferociously at her and barked, "So why the hell didn't Eric adopt you?"

She understood his anger. It wasn't directed at her, or even at Eric, just at circumstances he'd probably never realized existed. In the protected world he'd grown up in, they didn't. "It's okay, Ren. My life wasn't so bad. I adapted, and being adaptable is a real asset. Eric didn't adopt me, because in those days single people couldn't adopt.

Especially not single men. But he was there for me. Whenever I could sneak away from Ma Jensen, I'd go to Eric. He taught me to ski, gave me my first set of skis—secondhand bangy-boards with bindings that had to be reset after nearly every run. But they were all mine."

"Did I misunderstand, or didn't the Jensens run Elephant Mountain as a ski resort?"

"They did."

"And they didn't provide their foster children with gear to use?"

"Ren . . . we weren't there to be children," she explained with a gentle kindness that brought the sting of tears to the backs of his eyes. "We were there to bus tables and wash dishes and shovel snow. We went to school because the law insisted they send us, but except on days when a caseworker might show up, we got up early in the morning, did our chores for three, sometimes four hours, went to school, came home and worked as unpaid labor for the Jensens until ten or eleven at night. It got worse as we got older.

"When I arrived June was eleven and Sarah was twelve. They had the worst of it, but Kevin and I grew into it too."

"Couldn't your caseworkers do anything about it?"

She laughed, meeting his distressed gaze, and patted his hand. "Hey, don't look so depressed. I survived, didn't I? And look at me now. When I was finally able to break free of the system and get a paying job, I had more experience working at all sorts of hotel or resort jobs than most sixteen-year-olds. It was probably good for me. The welfare people thought so. They said all kids had to do dishes and clear tables and sweep floors, and I should be grateful for having a good home. Phrased that way, it made sense."

"Jeeze!" Ren was not impressed by the social workers' logic. "Didn't they realize there were degrees of doing dishes and clearing tables? How about your marks in school? Didn't they reflect the fact that you must have been exhausted and without time to study?"

"Who expects good marks from welfare brats?" she asked.

"I guess." He shook his head rapidly. "If you had enough moxie to run away at the age of eight, why didn't you run away again . . . and again if necessary, until they paid attention to your complaints?"

"In a word—Eric. If I'd run away, I'd have had to leave him behind. But when he got fired a few years later, I did just what you said. I ran away, again and again and again, until I was declared incorrigible and put into a state home for children. It wasn't a lot worse, and I was only there until I was sixteen. Then, I took off."

"And got a job in a hotel?"

She slithered down in the bed, and he followed her, snuggling her tight against him. Resting her head on his shoulder she said, "Not right away. I worked in a diner for a few months, then in a slightly better restaurant doing dishes and busing, then waiting tables." She yawned widely but continued.

Fascinated, he listened while she quickly outlined the rest of her early life. At the age of eighteen she began a search for her natural parents. With the help of a kind and wise woman named Judge Henry, she finally admitted she was never going to find out any more information than what she and the judge had uncovered, and that if she wanted a home she was going to have to create one for herself.

"I fell in love when I was twenty," she said, her voice quiet. "I was working as a night clerk in a hotel and going to college in the day. The man I loved, Mark, was in one of my business classes. He loved me too. And his parents liked me. Then they found out about me. After that, they didn't like me anymore. In time, Mark caved in to the pressure. That was when I got onto the train," she said quietly. "I had to leave. I didn't care where I went, so long as it was far, far away from anyone who knew about me. Ren, those people *investigated* me. It was awful. They made me feel so . . . dirty.

"I ended up in California and got a job with the Harbison chain of hotels and continued to go to school. When I had my degree in hotel management, the captain gave me the job I had when you and I first met, assistant manager of the Westmount Marina Hotel."

She was silent for several moments. When he didn't say anything, she opened her eyes, lifted her head, and looked at him. He was watching her solemnly. He still made no comment. Lowering her head again and letting her eyes fall shut, she said, "And there you have it. The full life history of Jacqueline Elliot Train."

"Knight," he said, when his throat could form the word.

She snuggled closer. "Yeah. 'Night, Ren."

He thought about telling her that she'd misunderstood him, but her breathing told him she was drifting to sleep. He lay holding her for a long time, stroking his hand from her shoulder to her hip, breathing in the scent of her. He kissed her closed eyelids, her cheeks, her nose, and then, very softly, her lips. Looking down at her he saw her lips curve into a smile and knew she had felt his kiss even while she slept.

Reaching out, he turned off the light and, still holding her, slid into sleep himself.

When he awoke, she was gone from the bed and the chalet was silent. He got up quickly, checked the small house, then looked for her skis and found them missing. Far across the flats he could see the chairs of the lift curving around out of the shack and swinging up, up, up, each one empty. He knew where she had gone.

The frosty air stung Renny's nose and burned his eyes, but there was a freshness about it that was heady as he skied off the chair and down the ramp, seeing only one set of tracks across the deep powder. Silently he followed them. She was sitting, skiless, on a snow-covered rock, looking at him expressionlessly.

"I thought we had a date," he said, kicking free of his skis and sitting down beside her in the snow.

She gazed out across the valley below toward the fiery sky in which the sun had not yet risen.

"I wasn't sure you'd want to keep it," she said after a few moments.

Removing his gloves, he cupped her face in his hands, tilting it up so the first slanting rays of sunlight gilded her thick, dark lashes. She blinked, but continued to look at him, and he read the misery in her eyes, felt it deep in his soul.

"You think I don't like you anymore now that I know about your background," he said as a statement not a question. "You think I've closed another door in your face, locked you out."

Her smile was crooked. Once more, he had surprised her with the depth of his understanding. "You wouldn't be the first one," she said.

"No, I realize that, but I still . . . like you, Jac. And want you," he added in a voice that was not quite steady.

Again, she hid her feelings behind her usual cheerful smile and said, "Thanks. That's good to know, Ren." She was going to say something else, but suddenly her throat closed off. A huge weight grew and grew in her chest, and, to her utter horror, the pain she had been holding in broke loose, translating itself into deep, uncontrollable sobs that shocked her as much as they shocked him. She never cried. Oh, heaven help her, she never did. So why now? She fought to stop herself, but the spasms overwhelmed her and came spilling out noisily as she clasped her fists under her chin, tight against her throat in a vain attempt to hold the weeping back.

"Oh, Lord!" Renny said, reaching for her, holding her. Swiftly he lifted her, placed her on his lap, and enfolded her in his arms, rocking her as if she were a child.

"Don't," he said, his voice cracking. "Ah, babe, don't! I love you, Jacquie!" The words were torn from him by a force as powerful as the one that was ripping the sobs from her. "I love you so damn much, and it kills me to see you so unhappy."

"Oh, Renny, don't say things like that," she said between sobs. "You don't love me. You feel sorry for me, and I can't bear it. You shouldn't have come. You'd better leave now. I'll stop in a minute. . . ."

But her crying continued, and even though he knew she didn't believe him, he told her again. "I love you. Jacquie, please, believe me, it's going to be all right. Don't cry, Jac. Don't! Everything will be fine." But he didn't know what he meant exactly, saying it was going to be all right. What was? Her life? His? He didn't know, so all he could do was hold her and try to tell her with the strength of his arms, the protection and warmth of his embrace, that he meant to see to it that nothing ever hurt her again.

How terrible it must have been to grow up never knowing from one day to the next where "home" was going to be—never knowing if the door you'd stepped out of in the morning would be locked against you in the evening. He remembered their jigsaw puzzle and her way of doing it. Boundaries. Borders. Structure. If you don't know where you came from, how can you possibly know where you are? Her only frames of reference were what she had created for herself. She needed clear definitions in her life. Yes or no. An insider or an outsider. A member of the family or a stranger. Loved or unloved. Wanted or unwanted.

How different her childhood had been from his. He had considered himself, while not a deprived child, most certainly an unhappy one. Unhappy? In light of what he'd learned about her past, he hadn't even begun to know the meaning of unhappy. Sure, he'd been forced into too tight a mold from too early an age. He had gone from the firm discipline of the nursery and his nanny to the even harsher constraints of military school.

But he had broken free, led his life as he chose to lead it. He accepted no limits. No slope was too steep, no contest too difficult, no ocean too threatening. When it was offered to him, he reached out and took his dream, knowing it might well cost him his family. At the time, if he'd thought about it, no doubt he would have counted the cost as cheap. Now he knew better. He knew that it was his family and the protective structure they'd formed, that had given him the personal strengths to rebel. If he'd grown up without structure, like Jacquie, would he, too, have to start a puzzle on the outside and work in? Require perimeters to keep himself safe?

What a strange world, he thought. A man who had rebelled against structure had fallen in love with a woman who needed just that to make her complete.

The depth of her deprivation appalled him. He'd always found adventure in moving on to other places. For her, new places must have held nothing but terror. For her, they'd been the frightening unknown, where total darkness would reign at night.

He frowned and stroked her hair, laid his cheek against her head, and decided he didn't approve of a world where an eight-year-old would consider stealing and smoking cigarettes a commonplace event, even a way of life. He approved even less of a world where a naked newborn could be abandoned in the back of a taxi. Hell, the man responsible for leaving her could just as easily have chosen a dumpster instead of the cardboard box she called her 'first home.'

Her home . . . Oh, Lord. Where did she call home now? He cradled her close, his heart aching. What was wrong with this world? he wondered bitterly. How could a warm and sensitive woman come to believe that she should make her home in a hotel, so the door could never be locked against her?

He had no answers. Not even for the biggest question in his mind: What was he going to do about her?

He didn't know, so he could only hold her while she wept. A long time later the terrible heaving of her body stopped. He continued to stroke her hair back from her face, watching an endless procession of empty chairs come swinging to the top of the mountain, pivot around the stanchion in the shed, and then disappear down over the other side of the hill. He watched, because he knew that sooner or later one of those chairs would be occupied, and he wanted to be able to warn her. Jacqueline, he knew, would not care to be seen by a guest or an employee, weeping in the arms of a man—not even if he was her husband.

Before he was forced to disturb her, she lifted her head, wiped her eyes on the wadded tissue she dug from a pocket, blew her pink nose, and slipped down from his lap. Without looking at him, she put her skis on, adjusted her gloves and goggles, and slid her hands into the grips of her poles. Lifting her tips to start her glide through the thick powder, she glanced at him over her shoulder.

"Renny?" Her voice was husky.

"Yes, Jac?"

"Don't . . don't think that makes me *your* creature, okay?"

He frowned for a minute before he remembered what she was talking about. Eric. Her first lap. Oh, Lord, did that mean his was only her second? He wanted to haul her back onto it and hold her there, tell her it was her place and no one could ever kick her off. But she didn't want to know that any more than she wanted to know he loved her. He just nodded. "Okay. I won't."

As he paralleled her wide sweeps down the mountain, he knew beyond a doubt, he had become hers.

Nine

By the time they reached the bottom, the ascending lifts were filled with skiers. At the base of the T-bar, Renny's first class of the day was lined up and waiting for him. He skied to a halt a hundred yards away from them, cutting Jacquie off. A deft maneuver put his skis outside hers, his body close, and his hands on either side of her face.

Before she could take evasive action, he lifted her goggles so she couldn't hide behind them. Bending, he covered her mouth with his quickly, sweeping his tongue across her lips for just an instant, conveying a promise in his touch, and a plea. Letting her go, he said quietly, "I meant it, Jac. I love you."

Her aqua eyes flared with hope for an instant, but then she said, "You do not!" Glaring, she pushed with her poles and scooted backward from him. She turned and skied away as if she feared he would give chase. Behind her, she heard his low, triumphant laugh. "Oh, yes I do!" he shouted after her. "And tonight, I'll make you believe me."

All day she was itchy and antsy and cross. One minute she wanted to hide and cry some more, the next she'd find herself grinning like a fool. To nullify her swings of good humor, she'd frown until her head ached, and when Mai spoke to her, she snapped in response until the girl was near to tears as well.

All the while, in the back of Jacquie's mind, a little voice kept asking, *what if it's true?* Even if Ren believed it was true, she knew better. But, oh Lord, what if? Where did that leave them? What would it mean?

She tried to force herself to stay away from the window but found herself swiveling her chair around more often than she liked, her eyes sweeping the slopes looking for one distinctive blue ski suit that was the exact same shade as his eyes. What had he meant when he said that tonight he'd make her believe it? Oh, lordy, she knew exactly what he meant, and her entire body surged with desire at the thought. She wouldn't allow him to make her a victim of . . . of . . . biology! she decided. If he really loved her, if he meant to stay with her, then it would be different. She couldn't shake the feeling, however, that he was going to leave. When the mood struck him, he'd just up and go.

Still, last night hadn't she asked him to share her bed, not just once but on a continuing basis? She had, and she'd meant it. She hadn't been able to think of not having him with her every night. So what was changed now? She didn't know, but something had, and it was all because he'd said he loved her when he didn't, when all he really felt was pity.

She sent Mai home early because it was snowing hard and she didn't want her driving down the snowy mountain after dark. At least that's what she told Mai. In truth, she wanted privacy so she could think and not have to worry about being caught staring idly into space when she should have been concentrating on the huge stack of work on her desk. At seven o'clock, she called down to the cafeteria to order something to eat. At seven-fifteen, Elsie brought her a tray and a message from Renny to get home quick. Elsie laughed. She thought it was precious and funny and sweetly romantic.

Jacquie did not laugh.

Absently, she nibbled at her hamburger, ate a few French fries, poked a fork in and out of her cole slaw, and shoved the whole mess into the garbage. She drank endless cups of coffee from the big pot Mai had left for her, and when she was so tired her eyes were crossed, she finally got up and prepared to go home—then stopped and cleaned off the top of her desk, rubbing its surface to a gleaming finish with lemon oil.

She stood in the road scanning the empty hill, gazing through the swirling snow at the few lights still on in the lodge, at the halos around all the outdoor lights, and the muted glow of the lights in her own chalet. She sighed, knowing she could procrastinate no longer. She had to go home. Maybe by now he'd have realized he hadn't been totally honest. Maybe he was asleep in his own bed. Maybe he wasn't asleep in his own bed but was sitting up waiting for her. Waiting to tell her he'd made a mistake. Her stomach churned. Her throat hurt. Her eyes stung. She was shivering. And it wasn't even all that cold tonight.

The door was unlocked. Inside it was warm, although a heap of glowing coals behind the glass doors of the stove suggested that Renny had gone to bed a while ago. But where? she wondered. Silently she shut herself into the bathroom and emerged ten minutes later, showered, dried, and wrapped in a robe. Just as silently, she slipped past Ren's bedroom door and climbed the stairs.

With a shuddering sigh she recognized as relief, she found him in her bed. She slipped out of her robe and curled herself close against his back, one arm over his waist, one knee behind his legs. He murmured something unintelligible and turned to her, wrapping her in his arms, one hand pressing her cheek against his chest. "Jac . . . my Jacqueline . . ." he said with such deep satisfaction and a sigh of such perfect contentment, all at once she believed him. If he could speak to her in those tones, hold her with so much tenderness even while asleep, then she must believe the words he spoke when he was awake. No one could have faked the love she'd heard in his voice. Tears swam in her eyes, but she smiled against his bare, warm chest.

"I love you too," she whispered softly, and soon was asleep.

Jacquie awoke with a sneeze coming on and rubbed her nose without opening her eyes. The sneeze receded, then returned, a tickling sensation she could not ignore, and she wrinkled her nose. Coming more fully awake, she felt Renny's long warmth beside her and let her eyes flutter open. She smiled, sweet sensations prickling all over her skin, making her heart thud harder as she rubbed her cheek against his hard shoulder.

"I fell asleep," he said. "And I promised to convince you of something very important."

He was propped on one elbow looking down at her. He held a feather in his hand, flicking it against her cheek.

She cradled his stubbly jaw in one hand and said, "You convinced me, Ren."

His smile was swift and crinkled the corners of his eyes. "Nope. I may have been asleep, but believe me, if anything of that nature had gone on, I'd have woken up."

She smiled. "That wasn't what it took, Ren."

"No?" He looked skeptical. "So what did it take?"

"Just you. Just the way you were when I got home last night. You were sound asleep, and still you said my name and turned over and held me as if you'd never let me go."

The joy in his eyes made her feel as if she had bestowed a gift on him. She knew tears were gathering in her eyes and blinked to clear her vision.

He stroked one hand down her arm. "I won't ever let you go."

"Ah, Ren . . ." Her breath was tremulous.

"Hey, I mean that too."

"I know you do. For now."

"Forever." When her expression of doubt didn't change, he rubbed her chin with the feather that had somehow escaped from her eiderdown comforter. "I can see I've got some more convincing to do."

In the dim light that came through the windows as day approached, he bared her body slowly, trailing the feather over her breasts and stomach and thighs, right down to her toes, and then started back up again, slowly.

She shivered from the cool air, from the delicious sensations his touch aroused, and from the look in his eyes, and soon her shivers were tremors of heated desire. Her voice shook with a blend of laughter and the reaction she was trying to contain, the pleasure she wanted to prolong. "Didn't . . . didn't I hear somewhere that feathers are kinky?"

"Uh-uh." Renny grinned. "Just erotic. Kinky is—"

"Never mind. I remember." She grinned and puffed the feather away from her lips as he prepared to begin the downward journey of lovely torment all over again. Pushing him down onto his back, she lifted herself up and found one of his flat, dark nipples within the curls of hair on his chest. She flicked her tongue across it and then pulled it between her lips while her hands moved freely over his body. She wanted to give him equal pleasure.

His breathing increased but he lay still. He asked, "Who's supposed to be doing the convincing around here?" But she ignored him and continued to run her lips over his chest, down his stomach, across his flanks, until he was shuddering and rigid as he fought for control. She showed no mercy until he grabbed her head and held it still, gasping, "Jac, don't. Stop. Give me a break. Come here and kiss me."

She slid slowly up his body until her lips were only inches from his but held herself away from him on stiffened arms.

"You mean you kiss women who haven't yet brushed their teeth?" she asked.

He rubbed a fingertip over her moist, rosy lower lip. "Never," he said, cupping one of her buttocks in his hand and sliding her lower body closer to his.

"Well, then, let me get up and do it," she told him, her eyes half-closed as she enjoyed the sensation of his hard arousal against her thigh. "Because I mean to be well and truly kissed before I start to be convinced." She also wasn't at all sure of the status of her birth control protection after so many hours.

"You're going to be a helluva lot more than kissed, let me tell you." As she had done to him, he placed one hand on her shoulder and tipped her over onto her back, then held her pinned as he grabbed her head in both hands, looking deeply into her eyes. She forgot about everything but him.

"I don't kiss women," he said. "Not anymore. Just one woman. My woman. Jac—"

"Hush," she said quickly. "I know you wouldn't go with any other women as long as we're together. You don't need to tell me that, Ren. Just as I won't—"

"You're damned right you won't!" he cut in roughly, taking her mouth with hard, possessive force, slanting his own across it, parting her lips with one sure thrust of his tongue, an evocative motion that set her senses aflame. Her hips surged toward his. She had to get closer. One of her legs hooked up and over his waist and he groaned, dragging her even nearer, his hardness finding the soft, moist core of her, and he thrust deeply inside her welcoming body as she was swept up in a wave of wild passion.

"Yes! Yes!" she cried, as the waves began washing over her, the tension within her coiling tighter and tighter until it finally burst into cascading showers of delight. As swiftly as it had risen, it peaked for them both and receded, leaving them limp and weak and panting.

"Jacqueline," he said when he lifted his head. "Jacqueline, love, I was greedy and careless. Why didn't you tell me to stop?" he asked softly, apologetically.

"Who? Me?" she whispered, placing tiny kisses on his throat, down his chest. "I didn't want you to stop. You make me so crazy with one touch that I think I won't be able to stand it when you make me wait. Ren, you're fantastic. But I thought you didn't kiss women with dirty mouths?"

He laughed as he tilted her face up to look into her eyes. "Have you got a dirty mouth?" he asked. "I never knew. Talk dirty to me," he added in an insinuating tone.

Sliding up, straddling his body, she bent and whispered in his ear. For several moments he listened in silence and then playfully thrust her away, staring at her, pretending shock.

"Where did you ever hear about things like *that*?"

She grinned. "I made them up. I have a vivid imagination. If you're not interested . . ." She slipped out of his grasp and shot out of the bed, leaving him tangled in the bedclothes as she ran down the stairs and leaped into the shower, turning on the taps without much care about the temperature of the water. Luckily she didn't scald herself or freeze, and when Renny slid in beside her, the temperature was exactly right.

It turned out he was interested, and his imagination was just as vivid as hers.

They were both late for work.

"What do you mean you don't have any?" Ren crawled out from under the tree, long pine needles clinging to his flannel shirt and sticking out of his hair. With one arm, he reached into the branches, grasped the trunk, and gave it a quarter turn before stepping back to survey the results. "Come on, Jac. You must have collected *some* over the years."

"None. Not a single one. Why should I? There's always a Christmas tree in the lobby. Why do I need one here?"

"Dammit, Jacqueline, this is your home—our home. Of course we have to have a tree. And we need lights and silver bells and colored balls and tinsel and an angel for the top. Come on, we can make it to the hardware store in Marsden if we hurry. They're open till nine tonight, aren't they?"

"Ren!" she protested. "I just got home from work. I'm tired. I want some dinner."

He grabbed her jacket and flung it at her, then stamped into his boots. "You can rest in the car and we'll have dinner in the mall. Well? Come on."

Laughing, she put on her coat and boots and followed him out the door. In his Blazer, she snapped her seat belt around her and looked over at his intent, handsome face. A wave of tenderness washed over her. He looked like a little kid who was determined to get what he wanted.

"This is really important to you, isn't it?"

He shot her a glance as the Blazer bumped over the icy ruts in the parking lot then out onto the smoothly plowed road. "Of course it's important. It's Christmas."

She couldn't help but smile. "And so we have to decorate a tree?"

"Right. What else would we put all our gifts under? What else would we hang our stockings beside, since we can't hang them too close to the stove? And what else could make the house smell so good? Do you know how to bake gingerbread men?"

She was laughing helplessly by then. "Renny! No, I do not know how to bake gingerbread men! How many presents do you expect, anyway? You intend to hang up a stocking? I'm afraid you're in for a disappointment. Hasn't anybody ever told you there's no Santa Claus?"

He reached across the wide front seat and undid her seat belt, sliding her right over beside him, holding her tightly against his warmth. For just an instant his lips brushed over her cheek. "I know that's what you think, Jacqueline Train, but have I got news for you. This year, little girl, you're gonna find out there is one. Now do up your belt and stay close to me, okay? Why do you think they put one in the middle?"

Wordlessly, she did as she was told.

"Jac?" he asked a few minutes later. "You did

have a Christmas stocking when you were a child, didn't you? Every year?"

"Of course I did, dummy. None of the people I lived with were complete ogres, you know."

"No. I don't know." Only ogres, he thought, could let a child go once she'd been in their home for a few weeks or months, and Jacquie had been in seven different homes in her first four and a half years. How many others, he didn't know. He only knew that the one she'd stayed in the longest had been run by people he definitely considered ogres . . . *complete* ogres.

"What was the nicest Christmas present you ever had as a child?"

"Oh, that's easy. *The Miracle Worker,*" she said softly. "Eric gave it to me the year I was twelve."

"What's that?"

"A book. The story of Helen Keller. Since I hadn't been born deaf and blind—for a few weeks I felt cheated because of that—I decided the next best thing to being like Helen Keller was to be like her teacher, Annie Sullivan. For about six months that was my ambition in life."

"Then what happened?"

"Ambitions change," she said shortly, and he knew he was trespassing on emotional territory again. Of course, he realized. She had gotten the book from Eric when she was twelve. She'd run away when she was thirteen, after he got fired. What had her ambition been then? To find the one person who had made her feel she belonged somewhere? To find the only lap she had ever sat on?

"What was your favorite Christmas present?" she asked, and he was almost ashamed to reply. Hers had been a book. And his?

"A sailboat."

"When you were a child? You were a little kid and you got a sailboat? A real one?"

"A real one. A sleek, pretty little racing dinghy that even a child could handle alone. I was nine."

"And did you?" she asked after a moment's thought. "Handle it alone?"

"Sure I did."

"Your dad taught you how to sail?"

"Nope. He hired a guy to give me lessons, and when I passed I was free to go out alone."

"Alone," she said sadly, cuddling his arm to her cheek. "Oh, poor little boy."

He was startled by her statement and said, "I was not! I was a rich little boy."

"But probably just as lonely in your way as I was in mine. Renny? You know, I've envied you your family. I've thought you were sort of a louse for despising them the way you do. Were you alone an awful lot?"

"Yeah, I guess so. Only during vacations, though. Other times, when I was at school, I had lots of people around me. Sometimes too many. But we were talking about Christmases. What was the best stocking stuffer you ever had?"

She laughed. "Oh, come on! Who remembers things like that?"

"Kids do."

"In case it has escaped your notice, I am not a child." Deliberately, she moved her breast against his arm, and he laughed softly.

"No, ma'am, I'll certainly have to agree with you. But I still bet you remember the best stocking stuffer you ever got, so tell me."

"A red fuzzy hat. It was hooked over the top of a candy cane sticking out of the top of my stocking, and it was the prettiest, most elegant thing I had ever seen. It had a pom-pom on top, and it was brand-new. I adored it. I was seven, I think. Red was my favorite color."

Oh, hell, she'd done it again. A hat. A brand-new hat. Not a hand-me-down one. He wanted to cry for her, for the little girl she had been, for the things she'd never had. He wanted even more to make sure that she always had everything she wanted from here on out. When was she going to admit to him—as well as to herself—that she loved him? He told her of his love at least twenty times a day, but never once had she ever said the words back to him. Sometimes he doubted she ever would, or could, and always the thought was in the back of his mind: Maybe she didn't love him.

"What about you? Your favorite stocking stuffer?" she asked, breaking in on his thoughts.

He sighed and wished he'd never started this game. "A watch that worked to a three-hundred-foot depth," he said, wondering if it made her feel as bad as it made him feel to know her fuzzy red hat was being compared to a four-hundred-dollar watch. Or maybe she had no idea that when his parents bought watches, they didn't spare any cost. No, of course, she wouldn't know. He had nothing to be ashamed of. Only—he was ashamed.

"Did you dive when you were a child too?"

"No. It was just that a diver's watch was the most coveted item in my crowd of friends that year. I was eleven. What was your biggest Christmas disappointment?" If she told him, then he could tell her about the year he had managed to convince himself he was getting a puppy for Christmas. He'd thought if he had a dog to look after, his parents wouldn't be able to send him away to boarding school.

She thought for a moment and then said, "I never had one." He realized that it was probably true. When you learn from a young age not to expect anything, you're never disappointed. Her answer effectively put an end to the conversation. A few minutes later they arrived at the mall.

In the small shopping center on the outskirts of Marsden, Renny took her hand and together they wandered from store to store, browsing, laughing over silly things, sneaking kisses and hugs. They finally bought strings of lights, boxes of multicolored ornaments, tinsel and silver icicles, bells, and one shining star for the top.

"No angels?" Renny demanded of a harried clerk. "Whaddya mean, no angels?"

They were too late. All the angels were gone, and Jacquie wondered if wishing on a Christmas star was the same as wishing on any other star. If it was, she decided, looking at his crestfallen expression, she'd wish for just one more Christmas with Renny so she could provide him with an angel for the top of his tree.

His sulk was short-lived, and he forgave the poor clerk for having run out of angels. Wishing her a merry Christmas, he shoved their shopping cart, which was laden with boxes, out of the store.

"Why don't you take those things out to the car, and I'll meet you in the restaurant in, say, half an hour," Jacquie suggested. She had shopping to do and didn't want him around to see what she bought. A stocking, Lord, she had never thought he'd want to hang up a stocking. What in the world did you put in a Christmas stocking for a grown man?

It took her longer than she'd expected, and when she staggered into the restaurant, dragging her bags, Renny was waiting. By the look of the bags he had stacked on one of the chairs, though, he hadn't been waiting long. As she took off her coat, she caught him peering inside one of her bags.

"You cut that out!" she said. "No sneaking peeks, you cheat."

"Why can't I look? Is it for me?"

"No, it's not for you. Why would I buy something for you?"

He grinned. "I bought something for you. Aren't you the least bit curious?"

"Nope. Can we eat now? I'm hungry."

"What you are is inhuman," he said when she

moved all her parcels well out of his reach. "Will you let me squeeze and shake the boxes when you've got them wrapped?"

"Ren, I bought myself some new underwear and some tea towels for the kitchen. I picked up a few toys for the day-care room, and some gifts for Mai's children. Okay?"

He didn't believe her. All the way home he prodded her. "Just a hint. What did you get me?"

"I told you. Nothing. You're not a child. Christmas stockings are for kids."

"I guess you must be a kid, because you're going to have a stocking. I got lots of neat stuff to fill it with. Your favorite color is still red, isn't it? It better be." When she merely nodded, he said impatiently, "Jacqueline, that was a hint, you know! Now you're supposed to ask what I got you that's red."

Enjoying herself immensely, she said, "But why? I don't want to know." Though he fussed and carried on, she refused to play his game, having more fun with her own.

She had to admit that the tree did make the house smell heavenly, and when it had all its lights and other decorations on it, it gave the room a festive look. She curled on the couch and sipped wine Renny had poured for her, lifting her glass when he clicked his against it.

"To our first Christmas," he said, his gaze holding hers.

"Renny . . . don't."

"Don't what?"

"Don't . . . pretend."

He clicked their glasses together once more and then tilted hers to her lips, holding it there until she sipped. "What makes you so sure I'm pretending?"

She smiled. "None of this is real, Ren. We both know it." She waved a hand to include the tree, the wreath of holly and ivy he'd bought in the supermarket and hung on the door, the little bit of plastic mistletoe over the doorway between kitchen and living room. "We're . . . playing house, like little kids. You be the dad and I'll be the mom, and we'll decorate a tree and make believe it's Christmas. Okay. I'm willing to go along with you, but I won't pretend it will include more Christmases. This is it, Ren—all we'll have, all we'll want."

He sat on the floor and leaned his shoulders back against the couch near her knees. "Is it?"

"Of course. Ren, stop. I know what you're trying to find out. You aren't exactly being subtle, you know. I'm not going to let the sentimentality of one Christmas make me start begging for more. I won't read things into what you're doing that aren't there. I'm grateful to you for wanting us to have a wonderful season together, but come the end of April, we'll both be out of here."

"But . . out of here together," he said softly.

"Hey, Ren, I know better. I . . . snooped one day. I saw your sketches. You're designing a new boat. You're going sailing again."

"Oh, honey . . ." He drained his glass and set it down, then got to his feet, towering over her. "Yes, I'm designing a boat, boats. I've been having conversations with Runyon and Gray."

She raised her brows. "*Damon* Runyon and *Zane* Grey?"

His grin flashed. "No, bookworm," he said, tousling her hair and then crouching before her. "Clarissa Runyon and Edward Gray. They're boat designers and builders. They've offered me a job. I want to take it, but I told them I was committed here until the end of April." He looked into her eyes. "And I said I had to discuss it with my wife. So, let's discuss it, Jac. What about you? Where do you go when this place closes down?"

"Back home," she said. "At the beginning of the season when I came up here, Captain Harbison promised me something." She smiled, glowing with happiness. "If I increased occupancy here by one third, he'd give me the Westmount to run on my own." She drew a deep breath. "As of the end of January, if all the reservations are confirmed, I'll have done it! The Westmount, Ren. Just think!"

"The Westmount? In San Diego?" Dismay rang out in his voice. She looked closely at him. His face was losing color. He was very white as he slumped down beside her.

"Yes. It's what I've always wanted, what I've been working toward for years. And once it's mine, I'll never have to leave again. Someone else will run this place. Renny? Don't you think it's wonderful?"

He said nothing, only sat there looking stunned, miserable. "Isn't it great?" she asked.

"Sure, honey. It's . . . great." He smiled, his expression devoid of emotion. "I'm proud of you. The Westmount's the biggest resort in the Harbison chain, isn't it?"

She frowned. "Renny, what's wrong? Are you afraid I'll get in your way back in San Diego? I promised you I wouldn't ask for anything permanent. We can . . . terminate this agreement whenever you say."

"Oh, Jac!" He groaned and hauled her into his arms, burying his face against her hair. "I—no, dammit! I don't think it's great! I hate the idea of your living in San Diego, Jacquie, but only because Runyon and Gray are in San Francisco. Oh, love . . ." He tangled a fist in her hair and turned her face up to his. "Don't go there, Jac. Please. Come with me to San Francisco."

She stared at him. "Why?"

"Because I love you. I want to be with you. I thought I'd finally convinced you how I felt. Why is it so hard for you to believe that I love you? If I wasn't already married to you I'd propose, because I want to be with you for the rest of my life, but I don't think I can go back to San Diego, even for you. It's a prison to me, love."

She looked at him for a long time in silence, then said softly, "You would? Ask me to marry you? Oh, Ren! If you did, I'd say yes. I love you, and wherever we can both be happy is where I want our home to be." Her voice wobbled. "Our *home*, Renny . . ."

His hands tightened on her, his gaze became heated. "You love me? Jac, do you know what you said? Do you mean it?"

"I mean it. I fell in love with you two years ago. When you came back, my feelings got stronger and stronger. I know it will never end for me, but until now, I didn't think it would last for you. I thought you knew how I felt."

His laugh was of pure joy. "Oh, Jac, you never said it! How could I have known?" His voice throbbed with passion. "You never told me before. Of course you can't control it, I can't control the way I love you either. I don't want to. I only want to feel our love grow and grow—for the rest of our lives."

He swung her up into his arms as he stood, his gaze ardent, eyes flaring with love. "Remember what you said the day I came back, Jac? About a love so big that it couldn't be contained by just two people? Isn't that the kind of love we have? One so powerful we have to create another human being with it? Let me make a baby with you, Jac. Let me show you how big my love is!"

"Yes! Yes! Yes!" she cried, wrapping her arms around his neck as he carried her up the stairs. "Renny, I love you so much!"

When they were calm again, lying close together, warm and at peace, Ren slid the covers down and spread his hand over her belly. "Do you think we did it?"

She smiled. If ever a new human being had been created out of the vastness of two people's love, then they surely had done it.

He sat up and leaned over her. "Hey . . . you in there. I love you too." Bending lower, he kissed her abdomen as tenderly as he had ever kissed her lips.

Cradling her close, he murmured, "And even if we didn't, Jac, even if we never do, you and I . . . we're still a family, love, just the two of us."

Ten

"What time do we have to put in an appearance tomorrow?" Renny asked, nuzzling her ear as they danced to a dreamy number. He spun her back under the mistletoe hung in the middle of the lounge and kissed her. Around them, those slightly sodden revelers who noticed, clapped.

"Whenever," she said languidly. "I try to come before the brunch buffet is over, and it doesn't start until half past ten. It goes on until one-thirty. Why?"

"Because I have plans for tomorrow morning."

"Mmm? What plans are those?" She knew exactly what his plans were. For once, they could share an unhurried morning, loving, laughing, talking. She almost wished she didn't have a hotel to manage, to take up her time. It would be heavenly to be somewhere with Renny, alone, able to love when and where they chose. April . . . roll on, April! she thought.

"First," he murmured, "I'm going to wake you up the way you like best."

She lifted her head from his shoulder and blinked innocently. "Oh, good. With coffee?"

He treated her remark with all the respect it deserved, ignoring it completely. "And then," he went on, "I'll bring you your stocking and watch while you take out the goodies and enjoy them."

Again, she blinked at him. "Stocking? When did you start keeping the goodies in a stocking? Is that kinky or erotic?"

He snickered and said, "You'll see."

"So what comes after the erotic goodies you keep in a stocking?"

"The presents."

"Oh, I knew that," she said. "What I can't figure out is why we have to start out with them in a sock."

He lifted his arm and looked at his watch. "It's Christmas, Jacqueline. Right now it's Christmas, and I love you, and we had better get the hell out of here because if we don't, anybody who might be watching is going to go to bed with visions of more than sugar plums dancing through their heads."

Meeting his gaze, she said, "Take me home, Ren. I'm starting to have a few visions myself. Or maybe we should call them fantasies."

"Me too," he whispered, his eyes dancing with

delight. "Mine have to do with a naked dancer wreathed in mist in the middle of a snowy glade."

"Really?" She slipped out of his arms at the door of the lounge, and they walked hand in hand to where they had left their coats and boots. "I think I read somewhere that lovers should act out their fantasies. It's good for the relationship."

He laughed and held her coat for her, then shrugged quickly into his own. "Merry Christmas, everyone!" he shouted, and the two of them ran, laughing, eager, until they were halfway home. Coming to a halt, Renny turned her in his arms and said, "And merry Christmas to you, too, my love. The best one ever."

Fantasies, Jacquie had to admit, didn't always require exotic secret hot springs. One of hers was coming true where she stood.

Another came true in the morning—sharing a Christmas with someone special, someone who loved her, and whom she loved. They laughed over the silly things they'd put into each other's stockings, were touched by the lovely things they had found for each other, and beamed in thanks for the practical things. But when Jacqueline got to the last carefully wrapped gift Ren had tucked high in the branches of the tree, she opened it with trembling fingers, the size and shape of the box telling her what she would find.

"With this ring, I thee wed," he murmured as he slid the ruby-studded band onto her finger. "With all my worldly goods I thee endow."

"Oh, Ren . . ."

He kissed the tears from her cheeks. "I don't blame you for crying. I don't have a helluva lot of worldly goods to endow you with, love, but what I have is yours. Including my grandmother's house in Stinson Beach. It's old and big, and if you like it, we can keep it, live in it, fill it with children. But if you want something more modern, we can sell it. I promise, love, I'll work hard to make a good life for us. I may never be as rich as my father, but—"

"Renny . . . shut up." She plopped herself onto his lap and wrapped her arms around him. "Do you think I care about being rich? Do you think I care if our house is old? I only hope that we have enough money so I can stay home and raise our babies while they're little. I think that's so important, Ren."

"Me too," he said fervently. "No nanny, no day care, no boarding school. Just a mother and father who love them to pieces and are willing and able to show it." He kissed her for a long time, and then asked, "How many, Jac?"

"I don't think that's something we can decide right now," she said. "But let's make sure of the first one."

Laughing, he agreed, and tumbled her backward onto the couch.

It was the middle of February when they stood together in the bathroom. Jacquie was pale. Her hands trembled. Carefully, she dipped the small wand, and both of them stared at it, waiting. And then, her eyes streaming, mouth quivering, she tore her gaze from the wand and fixed it on Ren's face.

"It's turning pink, love! Oh, look, Renny, it's turned pink!"

Awed, he stared at the wand for another minute, and then looked at her glowing face. "Does that mean it's going to be a girl?"

She collapsed into his arms, all tangled up between laughter and tears. "No, dummy, it just means I'm pregnant for sure. Oh, Ren . . September. In September we'll have our first baby. Maybe on your birthday. Wouldn't that be fantastic?" Suddenly, the memory of her last pregnancy returned.

He held her fiercely. "We'll have the baby, Jac. This time we will."

She cupped a hand over her lower abdomen and pressed it there. Yes, she thought. This time it would be all right. She felt it with all her heart and soul.

Ren led her into the kitchen and poured them both coffee. "Will you tell Captain Harbison you're quitting?"

"Of course. I've suspected all along that the assistant manager's position he offered me at the Frobisher in Sausalito was a made-up berth for me, even though he was going to pay me the same as I get here. But . . . can we really do without what I earn?"

"We sure can. Honey, we won't be anywhere near the poverty line, and I want you to stay home just as long as you want to. If you choose to take a job, then we'll find a way to work things out, even if it means turning our house into a hotel."

She gaped. "It's that big?"

"Almost," he said with a grin. "With a few renovations it would make a first-class guest house."

"And you'd do that for me?"

"I'd do anything for you."

"I thought knowing you loved me made me happier than I ever deserved to be, but now . . . Oh, Ren, I've never been so happy in my life! I'm going to be taking on the job I've always wanted."

"But you're not going to do it alone," he said, sliding his hand up the sleeve of her bathrobe and wrapping her arm in his strong clasp. "I don't know how I could have left you in San Diego the way I did." He looked shaken. "But if I had stayed, I'd still be longing for my great adventure, because I'd have fallen in love with you and never gone."

"Renny, if you ever have a need for another great adventure, I want you to know you're free to take it. I hope our marriage will never seem like a prison to you."

He got up and leaned over her, grabbing a fistful of her hair and tilting her face back. "I think raising kids with you will provide plenty of adventure, Jacqueline Train. And fun, and laughter, and love."

"Mmm," she agreed. "Especially that."

"Uh, honey? Do you think we should? I mean . . . ?"

She stood and slipped her arms around his middle, pressing herself against him. "My books tell me stress is bad for pregnant women, and I'll be very, very stressed if you start trying to treat me as if I were made of marshmallows. Ren . . . love me."

He did. Once again, they were late for work. Few people noticed, however, and by the time the ski resort closed due to lack of snow in the middle of April, everyone was used to the new hours the manager and her husband kept.

"I don't see why we have to do this," Ren grumbled, slamming the door of the car and giving the key a vicious twist in the ignition. The engine of the Chrysler purred. "The drive will be too tiring for you. We should have told them no."

"Darling, the drive won't bother me a bit. I hate flying, Ren, so this is the only way. I'll be sitting down, won't I? And isn't that what you try to get me to do about eighteen hours a day? Besides, how could we possibly refuse? They're your parents."

He nodded glumly and put the car in gear, backing out of the carport at the side of their big old house. It was July, and the color-filled, bee-humming, perfumed garden that Jacquie tended and watered with such care blossomed around them, making leaving their home even more difficult. But soon the beauty of the ocean on their right compensated, as they drove beside it for several miles before turning inland.

"How many birthdays has my father celebrated

without my being present?" Ren continued to complain.

"I have no idea. But this year you are in a position to indulge him. It's only for a weekend, Ren. And I'm longing to see the captain." She grinned and patted her round belly. "I want to show off. I have a feeling Captain Harbison will be just as pleased as Eric is."

His hand moved hers out of the way so he could pat it himself. "All right. I guess I'm kind of looking forward to showing you off myself. I warn you, though, Jacqueline, the first time either of them says one thing about grooming another little architect to fill out the gap in the family firm, we're out of there. Okay?"

She held his hand under her own. "Renny, don't you know that they can't force our child into their mold any more than they were able to force you? He's going to have too much of you in him—and too much of me."

"He?" Renny glanced at her, his face losing its tense lines as he smiled. "Are we having a boy?"

"I hope so. Because that's what you want."

"You want a girl."

"Someday I'll have one, but this is your son in here, my love. I'm confident of that."

"Your confidence inspires me. I know you're right. Nothing my family can do or say will be able to hurt me again, not as long as I have you. Don't ever leave me, Jacquie. Promise me."

Swiftly, joyously, she promised him.

The drive did tire her. Long before they stopped

for the night, as Renny had insisted they must, her back was aching, even though he had stopped the car frequently and they had walked for exercise.

The next day's drive was not as long, but Jacquie was exhausted when they arrived in San Diego and Ren drove out into the undulating foothills of the Coast Range where his parents' home was located.

A swim in the pool refreshed her enough to enjoy an alfresco dinner, and afterward she sat on the patio under the strings of colored lights already in place for the next night's birthday party, sipping a soda and lime. The whole family was gathered, chatting, and Ren was at her side. She lay back on her lounge chair and listened idly to his brother-in-law, Clay Fisher, discuss his own importance to the architectural world and his wise investments. What Clay forgot to bring up, Ren's sister, Crystal, made sure he remembered, with help from both of her parents. At least no controversial subject came up and there was no dissent.

Ren had been wrong. This weekend was going to work out after all. She let her eyes fall shut, and when she felt herself being lifted and carried into the house, she never bothered to open them. She snuggled down into bed and slept.

The next day was filled with party preparations. Caterer's staff rushed around. Decorators added finishing touches to the already perfect—in Jacquie's opinion—house and grounds. Ren's mother twittered and fussed. Crystal sighed dramatically and declared that nothing was going to be ready on time, and if she weren't saddled with being the "only child her parents could rely on," things would surely go better. Jacquie and Ren escaped to spend the afternoon with Captain Harbison, basking in the glow of his approval.

"Are you looking forward to tonight?" Ren asked as he pulled their car into the garage at the rear of his parents' home.

"Not much," she admitted. "Why can't they just have family and some good friends over to celebrate with? Why do they have to go to so much trouble? This is almost as elaborate as their fortieth anniversary, isn't it? When your mother said they were having a little gathering at home, I was relieved, but they might as well have rented the entire Westmount again."

He laughed and tucked her hand under his arm as they wandered toward the house. "Now do you see why I hate their parties? My parents consider family and some good friends to number about three hundred people. But don't worry. There'll be so many people here that no one will bother us. We might even be able to sneak away to bed early."

"Sounds like heaven to me." Even though she had been sick only a few times in her pregnancy, Jacqueline could never get quite enough sleep.

Even spread out over the extensive grounds and through the rooms of the big, sprawling house, more than three hundred people made an incredible amount of noise.

Jacquie had been introduced to more "good

friends" than she would ever be able to remember, had shaken more hands and accepted more congratulations than ever before in her life. Her back hurt, her head ached, as did her feet and her face—the latter from forcing a smile.

"If I have to say, 'September twenty-fourth, and no, I have no preference as to a girl or boy,' one more time," she said to Renny with a laugh when they had found a secluded corner behind an oleander bush, "I'm going to scream. You'd think no one here had ever seen a pregnant woman!"

He pulled her more tightly against him and supported her back with his arm. They were sitting on the grass. "No one ever thought they'd see a woman pregnant with my child. That's the novelty, I think. They're probably all speculating as to how long our marriage will last." And some people, like his sister, Ren reflected, were hoping the marriage would fail. Of course, Crystal thought she had an ax to grind. Renny was taking a perverse pleasure in not telling her otherwise.

She laughed and snuggled against him. "We'll show 'em, won't we, Renegade?"

"Ain't no renegades in this family, lady. Just a steady, hardworking guy with a wife and baby to feed."

"Speaking of which, would you be kind enough to let me go on hiding here while you go and find me some food? I'm starving."

He got to his feet and grinned down at her. "When aren't you?"

"Um . . . never?"

"Well, maybe I'm being unfair. You don't seem to eat when you're engaged in your other favorite pastime. Are all pregnant women like you? Either eating or sleeping?"

She leaned back on her hands and smiled. "Seems to me there is one other activity I enjoy. I kind of thought you'd noticed, but maybe you haven't."

He looked at her through narrowed eyes. "I've noticed. In fact, I've been hoping you might stay pregnant for a lot longer than nine months, if that's the way it's gonna affect you." He took a step away, turned and came back. "Maybe the food could wait? Nobody would ever find us here."

"Get going! Anybody could find us here!"

Laughing, he left her, hurrying away, so that he could hurry back.

Jacquie was right. Anybody could find her hiding spot, but the one who did was Clay Fisher.

"Well, hello, there," he said. "I saw Renny coming out of here and wondered who he'd been dallying with. His wife! I'm amazed."

Her hackles rose. "Really? Why should that amaze you?"

"Well, clearly he's done what he had to." His gaze fell to her gently protruding abdomen. Instinctively, she cupped her hands around it, as if to shield it from his eyes. Clay Fisher was not a nice man, she thought. He had eyes she couldn't trust, and a personality she couldn't warm up to. She wished he'd go away, but he dropped to the grass beside her.

"Renny didn't 'have' to get me pregnant. We chose to have a child because we both want one badly."

"Jacqueline, tell that to the guests if you like, but don't forget, I'm family. Ren's no more obliged to stay with you now than he was after you got married. The marriage was all that was required then, the pregnancy is all that's required now—or its successful conclusion. Maybe he's sticking around to make sure you don't get rid of it."

Jacquie stared at him, feeling sick. "What?"

His laugh was unpleasant. "Tell me, what was Ren's reaction when he learned that he was going to have the heir he'd been supposed to produce? I know his parents were pleased when he told them. The old man all but ordered him to stick around up there in Canada and make sure you didn't have a chance to get rid of it."

"Clay, that's insane. Renny's 'sticking around,' as you put it, because he loves me and our child. You have no right to suggest otherwise."

Suddenly her quiet little corner behind the bush was no longer a haven. She got to her feet, ready to walk away. Like a snake, Clay's hand stuck out and captured her wrist.

He, too, rose. He lifted his brows. "Loves you, does he? Oh, sure, just like he loved you when he married you to get his hands on the first half of his grandfather's legacy. He loves your child in the same way and for the same reason."

She could hear the sounds of voices and music through the roaring in her ears.

"What do you mean?" *First half? Did that imply that there was a second half?* No. Renny would have told her.

"Don't you know? Didn't he tell you? In order to get the last half of his inheritance, Renny has to father a child by the same woman he married to get the first half—within five years."

She could feel the blood leaving her head, knew she was swaying and tried to steady herself. Clay's overly handsome face swam in front of her. His voice faded in and out. "I don't believe you," she said. "You're lying!"

"I'm not," he insisted. "Ask Ren. I . . . Oh, good grief, Jacqueline, listen, I'm sorry you didn't know. I had no intention of upsetting you. Look, you better sit down for a minute. No, wait—"

She didn't wait. She walked away, numb, her head whirling, her whole body aching as if it had been kicked. *The last half of his inheritance?* Oh, Lord, she couldn't bear it! Never had she felt such pain! She remembered how he had repeated her words back to her: *A love so big and so powerful, the only way to contain it is to create another human being with it.* He had used that need of hers for his own purposes, had lied when he said he loved her.

Her feet carried her into the house and down the corridor to their room. She picked up her purse and tucked it under her arm. Where was she going? She didn't know. She only knew that she had to get away before she was forced to see Renny again.

Partway along the sweeping, circular drive a car sat with its engine running and lights on. She snatched open the passenger door and stared in at the startled guest behind the wheel. "Please, if you're going into town, could I get a lift?"

He tried to talk to her, but if she responded, she wasn't aware of it. She must, however, have told him she wanted to go to the Westmount Marina Hotel, because he pulled up in the forecourt, and she dimly recognized where she was.

She staggered through the front door when the doorman swung it open for her. He frowned in alarm and took her shoulders in his hands. "Jacquie? Jac, what's wrong? You look like hell!"

"Nothing. I . . . need to see the captain. Is he in?"

"Sure. I'll unlock the elevator for you."

The elevator opened right into the penthouse, and the doorman must have phoned up in a hurry, because Captain Harbison was standing there waiting to catch her as she stumbled out and into his arms.

"Jacqueline, my dear, what is it?"

"Oh, Captain," she said with a moan. "I think I want to be dead."

Later, they talked, and it was like old times. Her teacher, her mentor in many ways, her savior during the days she'd suffered over Mark's weakness, Captain Harbison knew her well and cared for her like a daughter.

He heated up a can of tomato soup and made

her sip a cup of it. It went down smoothly, and it calmed her with its warmth.

"Why didn't you talk to Renny about it?" Captain Harbison asked. "It might not have been true, Jacquie."

"Oh, it's true," she said, anger not lessening her grief. "I don't doubt that for one minute. It was true about our marriage, wasn't it? He was willing to take a wife to inherit. Why shouldn't it be true that he'd go as far as to have a child, if there was a further stipulation to his grandfather's will? Clay had no reason to lie about it, and as much as I dislike him, I believe he truly didn't know that Renny hadn't told me. I could sense it, and I believe he was sorry he'd spoken out of turn."

Captain Harbison looked skeptical. He knew Clay Fisher by reputation. The man cheated at cards. He was unfaithful to his wife. How well could he be trusted? "I still think you owe it to Renny—and to yourself—to give him a chance to explain."

"I can't," she said, tears flowing again.

"All right, all right," Captain Harbison said, his expression softening. "I won't insist, not tonight. I think you should be in bed, my girl. Tomorrow will be soon enough. But, Jac . . . let me call Renny and tell him you're here? He'll be crazy with worry if I don't."

Sobs shook her, because she knew the captain was wrong, but she nevertheless nodded her permission. For the captain's sake, not for Ren's.

"But I don't want to talk to him no matter what he says, not under any circumstances."

"All right. I'll explain."

Jacquie refused the sedative Captain Harbison offered her and, with her knees pulled up and her arms wrapped protectively around her baby, she escaped into a deep sleep that didn't end until a bright ray of sunlight sliced into the room.

Instinctively she reached for Ren . . . and then remembered. She got up, stumbled into the bathroom, and was violently sick. Leaning against the basin, she slowly brought herself under control. "Renny . . ." she whispered. "Oh, Lord, how can I go on without you?"

She crept back into her bed and sat there, hearing Renny say, *Don't ever leave me.* Other words of his came to her mind. *Why is it so hard for you to believe that I love you? . . . I want to be with you for the rest of my life.* And, *Even if we never do have a child, you and I—we're still a family.* She played those words over and over and each time she heard them in her mind, she heard the throbbing sincerity, the deep love, that had colored his voice. He had meant each word. He hadn't been lying. Even if what Clay had told her was true, it didn't make a liar out of Ren, did it? No! No, of course it didn't. He'd have an explanation. She knew he would.

She showered and dressed and ran from her room. "Captain, could I . . ."

Without a word, and without waiting for her to

finish, he dangled a set of car keys in front of her nose. "This what you want?"

"Yes!" She kissed his cheek. "Thank you. Thank you so much."

"It's the maroon Mercedes," he said as the elevator doors slid open for her. "Are you able to drive?"

"I'm fine, Captain. Of course I am. In every way." She smiled. "And you knew I would be, didn't you?"

"I knew, Jac. There's good stuff in you. All you needed was a little sleep and to do a lot of thinking. Go get him, little girl, and take care."

Take care, she thought as she drove out into the hills. I will, Captain. I will take care of everything—of Renny, of myself, our baby, and our marriage. Because where there's enough love, other things don't matter.

"Gone?" Jacquie stared at her sister-in-law. "Gone where? When?"

"Back to San Francisco. Sometime last night. Your lack of consideration nearly ruined my father's party, Jacqueline. None of us appreciated it, especially Ren. Considering your background, however, I suppose there's no point in expecting more."

Jacquie scarcely registered Crystal's words. "Gone?" she said again. "But . . . without me? Did he leave any message?"

Crystal Fisher shrugged. "I'm sorry. Nothing."

Silently, Jacqueline opened the trunk of the

Mercedes so a gardener could load in her suitcases. Renny had left all her things neatly packed for her in their room. Clearly he thought she would be staying in San Diego. Did that mean he didn't want her in San Francisco? She struggled to keep a positive attitude and refused to think along those lines. He loved her. He wanted her. He had left without her because he was hurt. How badly had she hurt him by not trusting him? She had no way of knowing and could only hope he'd forgive her. She would convince him to—somehow. He had persevered and fought for her love; now, if necessary, she would do the same for his.

He must have driven all night. When the taxi let her out by the door, and she carried her bags in, he was standing in the middle of the living room, his face drawn and beard-stubbled, eyes red-rimmed. She sat her bags down and remained still, watching him, waiting.

"You're here? How did you get here so fast?"

"In a plane." She wondered if his blankness hid his pain, or simply indicated indifference. Suddenly the positive attitude she had forced herself to keep began seeping out, leaving icy terror in its wake.

"You don't like flying," he said harshly. "What was the rush, anyway? Did you hope to beat me home and be all packed and gone before I got here?"

"No, Ren. I wanted to see you. I wanted to tell you I'm sorry I ran out on you last night."

He blinked. "Yes. Well, I'm sorry you did, too, because it ruined something I figured was pretty wonderful."

She felt herself become light-headed. "Did it, Ren? Ruin it? Completely?"

He moved then, flopping into a chair near where she stood. "It was pretty hard to take, Jacqueline. I mean, you didn't ask me about it. You listened to Clay and then went flying out of there as if you were afraid of contamination. I would have appreciated a chance to explain."

"Yes. I know. So I came home to let you do that."

He might not have heard her. "Oh, I know I should have told you months ago, maybe even in the beginning, when we married, but I didn't think it would matter. I didn't see how you'd ever find out."

She swallowed so that she could speak. "I see. But Ren, I did find out, and I admit it hurt me—badly. That's why I ran. I was running from the hurt as much as from you. When I woke up this morning, I was more—sane. I took the time to think, the time to remember. And I knew you really loved me, that it hadn't been a lie just so I'd have a baby for you."

He rubbed a hand over his face. "Sure. Now that you've seen the lawyer, you know. What hurts me, Jac, is that you didn't know it without having to see him, without having to be told."

From a long way away, she heard her own voice. "What lawyer? Told what?"

He stared at her hard and got to his feet, concern all over his face. "Hey, lie down, will you? Damn, but you're pale! Jac, come on. Lie down!" He lifted her and put her on the sofa, his hands trembling as he straightened her legs out and put a pillow behind her head.

"Renny, dammit, what lawyer?" she demanded.

"The one whose name I left for you at the house."

"I . . . wasn't given the name of any lawyer."

"Didn't you see my mother? Or Crystal? They both promised if you came back, they'd give you my note."

She bit her lip. "I . . . talked to the gardener who put my bags in the car for me," she said evasively. *No message.* She had heard Crystal's words clearly. She had told her there was no message.

"Then . . . why did you come home?"

"Why? Because I love you and you love me, and we belong together. Ren, I've told you I'm sorry. I don't know what else to say. Forgive me, please. Because even if you tell me to get out, I'm staying. I will not give up on us. We're too important to let something tear us apart. Maybe the other half of your inheritance will make your life easier. Maybe you won't have to work so hard, so many hours a day. You need some time for fun, Ren. I know that. I—"

"You talk too much," he said, and covered her mouth with his own.

"Jac, I don't want the other half of my damned inheritance. I only want you and our baby," he said at last.

She drew in a tremulous breath and smiled. "Oh, love, I'm so glad to hear you say that! Thank you, Ren. Thank you. But . . . won't you have to take the money? When we've had the baby?"

"No," he said. "Not if I don't want it, and I don't. I won't be dictated to ever again, or bought, the way I let myself be bought when the old man died. You once told me you'd done a lot of thinking after you lost the other baby. Well, I did a lot, too, out there on the ocean. Though it took me a long time to admit it, I was pretty much ashamed of the way I let them manipulate me. What I should have done is told them to keep the old man's money and found a way to finance that trip myself." He paused, smiled, and then said, "But if I hadn't decided to fulfill the terms, I wouldn't have you, and I know I did the right thing now, even if I did it for all the wrong reasons."

"What happens to the other half of the money if you refuse it?"

"Jac, I intend to refuse it, but the lawyer says I can't make that decision until we have the baby and qualify legally. Why? Do you think I should take it? You're right, it might make our lives easier. If I refuse it outright, I guess it goes to Crystal, the way the whole thing would have done if I hadn't gotten married."

"I see," she said softly.

Renny smiled. "Yeah. Okay, what if we take it and donate it to . . . some worthy cause that really needs funding?"

"That sounds wonderful," she said. "What about

a home for unwed mothers, and care and counseling for after they have their babies? Would there be enough?"

He understood at once. "Of course. Maybe we could prevent what happened to you from happening to someone else."

She looked down at his big hand as he slowly unbuttoned her blouse, watching as he cupped her full breast, watching as the dark nipple rose to his touch. "Am I to take this as an indication that you've forgiven me for doubting your love?"

She could feel his smile as his bristly cheek pressed into her tender flesh—both the smile and the prickles felt wonderful. "Oh, no," he said, his voice a soft rumble. "You have a lot of penance to do, Jacqueline Train. Hours and hours and hours of it."

"Ummm . . . then I'd better get at it." She sighed happily.

"And keep at it too," he said.

So she did.

Epilogue

"There," Jacqueline said. "Now you can open your eyes."

Renny glowered at her. "Get down off that ladder, woman! Are you forgetting you're pregnant again?" He reached up and plucked her down, setting her firmly onto her feet on the floor.

"Don't you like it? I promised myself last Christmas, Ren, that if I was to be granted one more Christmas with you, I'd make sure you had an angel for the top of your tree."

He smiled. "And I promised myself last Christmas that we were going to be granted a whole lifetime of Christmases together. Jac, have I told you lately that I have everything I've ever wanted?"

He reached out and slid the baby seat a few feet closer, putting their three-month-old daughter, Jennifer, under the tree. "There," he said with satisfaction as he drew Jacqueline against his chest. "An angel on top, another one underneath, and the best one in my arms."

THE EDITOR'S CORNER

Have you been having fun with our **HOMETOWN HUNK CONTEST**? If not, hurry and join in the excitement by entering a gorgeous local man to be a LOVESWEPT cover hero. The deadline for entries is September 15, 1988, and contest rules are in the back of our books. Now, if you need some inspiration, we have six incredible hunks in our LOVESWEPTs this month . . . and you can dream about the six to come next month . . . to get you in the mood to discover one of your own.

First next month, there's Jake Kramer, "danger in the flesh," the fire fighter hero of new author Terry Lawrence's **WHERE THERE'S SMOKE, THERE'S FIRE,** LOVESWEPT #288. When Jennie Cisco sets eyes on Jake, she knows she's in deep trouble—not so much because of the fire he warns her is racing out of control toward her California retreat, as because of the man himself. He is one tough, yet tender, and decidedly sexy man . . . and Jennie isn't the least bit prepared for his steady and potent assault on her senses and her soul. A musician who can no longer perform, Jenny has secluded herself in the mountains. She fiercely resists Jake's advances . . . until she learns that it may be more terrifying to risk losing him than to risk loving him. A romance that blazes with passion!

Our next hunk-of-the-month, pediatrician Patrick Hunter, will make you laugh along with heroine Megan Murphy as he irresistibly attracts her in **THANKSGIVING,** LOVESWEPT #289, by Janet Evanovich. In this absolutely delightful romance set in Williamsburg, Virginia, at turkey time, Megan and Dr. Pat suddenly find themselves thrown together as the temporary parents of an abandoned baby. Wildly attracted to each

(continued)

other, both yearn to turn their "playing house" into the real thing, yet circumstances *and* Megan's past conspire to keep them apart . . . until she learns that only the doctor who kissed her breathless can heal her lonely heart. A love story as full of chuckles as it is replete with the thrills of falling in love.

Move over Crocodile Dundee, because we've got an Aussie hero to knock the socks off any woman! Brig McKay is a hell-raiser, to be sure, and one of the most devastatingly handsome men ever to cross the path of Deputy Sheriff Millie Surprise, in LOVESWEPT #290, **CAUGHT BY SURPRISE,** by Deborah Smith. Brig has to do some time in Millie's jail, and after getting to know the petite and feisty officer, he's determined to make it a life sentence! But in the past Millie proved to be too much for the men in her life to take, and she's sure she'll turn out to be an embarrassment to Brig. You'll delight in the rollicking, exciting, merry chase as Brig sets out to capture his lady for all time. A delight!

You met that good-looking devil Jared Loring this month, and next Joan Elliott Pickart gives you his own beguiling love story in **MAN OF THE NIGHT,** LOVESWEPT #291. Tabor O'Casey needed Jared's help to rescue her brother, who'd vanished on a mysterious mission, and so she'd called on this complicated and enigmatic man who'd befriended her father. Jared discovers he can refuse her nothing. Though falling as hard and fast for Tabor as she is falling for him, Jared suspects her feelings. And, even in the midst of desperate danger, Tabor must pit herself against the shadowed soul of this man and dare to prove him wrong about her love. A breathlessly beautiful romance!

Here is inspirational hunk #5: Stone Hamilton, one glorious green-eyed, broad-shouldered man and the hero of **TIME OUT,** LOVESWEPT #292, by Patt

(continued)

Bucheister. Never have two people been so mismatched as Stone and beautiful Whitney Grant. He's an efficiency expert; she doesn't even own a watch. He's supremely well-organized, call him Mr. Order; she's delightfully scattered, call her Miss Creativity. Each knows that something *has* to give as they are drawn inexorably into a love affair as hot as it is undeniable. Just how these two charming opposites come to resolve their conflicts will make for marvelous reading next month.

Would you believe charismatic, brawny, handsome, *and* rich? Well, that's just what hero Sam Garrett is! You'll relish his all-out efforts to capture the beautiful and winsome Max Strahan, in **WATER WITCH,** LOVESWEPT #293, by Jan Hudson. Hired to find water on a rocky Texas ranch, geologist Max doesn't want anyone to know her methods have nothing to do with science—and everything to do with the mystical talent of using a dowsing stick. Sam's totally pragmatic—except when it comes to loving Max, whose pride and independence are at war with her reckless desire for the man she fears will laugh at her "gift." Then magic, hot and sweet, takes over and sets this glorious romance to simmering! A must-read love story.

Enjoy all the hunks this month and every month!

Carolyn Nichols
Editor
LOVESWEPT
Bantam Books
666 Fifth Avenue
New York, NY 10103